"I'm looking for someone to pretend to be my wife," Jed began.

"So I heard."

"I was wondering if you'd take on the job."

Kristi's eyes widened in disbelief. "Me?"

He shrugged. "It was just an idea."

"But I heard you were looking for someone rich and sophisticated. This is me, remember? Good old Kristi."

"You don't have to *be* rich, you just have to look it." He ran his gaze up and down her slender figure. "You sure do look good in a dress."

She stared at him so long, he began to get worried. He was all set to say forget he ever asked. But he couldn't believe how hard he was hoping she'd agree.

And he wasn't sure how much that had to do with the fact that he couldn't seem to take his eyes off the smooth expanse of bare flesh beneath the lacing on her dress....

Dear Reader,

It's summer, the perfect time to sit in the shade (or the air conditioning!) and read the latest from Silhouette Intimate Moments. Start off with Marie Ferrarella's newest CHILDFINDERS, INC. title, *A Forever Kind of Hero.* You'll find yourself turning pages at a furious rate, hoping Garrett Wichita and Megan Andreini will not only find the child they're searching for, but will also figure out how right they are for each other.

We've got more miniseries in store for you this month, too. Doreen Roberts offers the last of her RODEO MEN in *The Maverick's Bride,* a fitting conclusion to a wonderful trilogy. And don't miss the next of THE SISTERS WASKOWITZ, in Kathleen Creighton's fabulous *One Summer's Knight.* Don't forget, there's still one sister to go. Judith Duncan makes a welcome return with *Murphy's Child,* a FAMILIES ARE FOREVER title that will capture your emotions and your heart. Lindsay Longford, one of the most unique voices in romance today, is back with *No Surrender,* an EXPECTANTLY YOURS title. And finally, there's Maggie Price's *Most Wanted,* a MEN IN BLUE title that once again allows her to demonstrate her understanding of romance and relationships.

Six marvelous books to brighten your summer—don't miss a single one. And then come back next month, when six more of the most exciting romance novels around will be waiting for you—only in Silhouette Intimate Moments.

Enjoy!

Yours,

Leslie J. Wainger
Executive Senior Editor

Please address questions and book requests to:
Silhouette Reader Service
U.S.: 3010 Walden Ave., P.O. Box 1325, Buffalo, NY 14269
Canadian: P.O. Box 609, Fort Erie, Ont. L2A 5X3

THE MAVERICK'S BRIDE

DOREEN ROBERTS

Silhouette®
INTIMATE™ MOMENTS®

Published by Silhouette Books
America's Publisher of Contemporary Romance

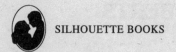 **SILHOUETTE BOOKS**

ISBN 0-373-07945-1

THE MAVERICK'S BRIDE

Copyright © 1999 by Doreen Roberts

This edition published by arrangement with Harlequin Books S.A.

® and TM are trademarks of Harlequin Books S.A., used under license.
Trademarks indicated with ® are registered in the United States Patent
and Trademark Office, the Canadian Trade Marks Office and in other
countries.

Visit us at www.romance.net

Printed in U.S.A.

Books by Doreen Roberts

Silhouette Intimate Moments

Gambler's Gold #215
Willing Accomplice #239
Forbidden Jade #266
Threat of Exposure #295
Desert Heat #319
In the Line of Duty #379
Broken Wings #422
Road to Freedom #442
In a Stranger's Eyes #475
Only a Dream Away #513
Where There's Smoke #567
So Little Time #653
A Cowboy's Heart #705
Every Waking Moment #783
*The Mercenary and the
   Marriage Vow* #861
*Home Is Where the Cowboy Is #909
*A Forever Kind of Cowboy #927
*The Maverick's Bride #945

Silhouette Romance

Home for the Holidays #765
A Mom for Christmas #1195
In Love with the Boss #1271
The Marriage Beat #1380

*Rodeo Men

DOREEN ROBERTS

lives with her husband, who is also her manager and her biggest fan, in the beautiful city of Portland, Oregon. She believes that everyone should have a little adventure now and again to add interest to their lives. She believes in taking risks and has been known to embark on an adventure or two of her own. She is happiest, however, when she is creating stories about the biggest adventure of all—falling in love and learning to live happily ever after.

To Bill,
who is, and always will be, my joy,
my life and my inspiration.

Chapter 1

Jed Cullen shifted his weight and resisted the urge to tug at the tie that threatened to choke him. If there was one place where he felt like a thistle in a field of daisies it was a wedding. Especially if he was all gussied up in a monkey suit and a tie that had taken a good half hour to coax into a bow.

He could feel the gaze of at least a dozen or so guests boring into his back as he stood next to his travel partner and best friend, Cord McVane. The room was small and elegant, not at all what he'd imagined a Las Vegas wedding chapel to look like.

Two gigantic vases of flowers flanked a low altar bearing three white candles, only one of which had been lit. A solemn-faced priest stood behind them and studied the guests as they took their seats.

Jed sent a sideways glance at Cord, who appeared to be miraculously unruffled, considering he was

about to become a married man. In fact, Cord didn't
seem like himself at all…it was as if he'd already
thrown off the restless life of a rodeo cowboy, and
was all set to take on the responsibilities of a husband.

Jed gave his head a slight shake, still unable to
believe that Cord McVane, of all people, had decided
to take the plunge into the unknown territory of mat-
rimony. First his buddy Denver Briggs, now Cord.
The three of them had gone through some tough
times together. Rodeo just wouldn't be the same
without them.

When he'd asked Cord why he'd chosen tuxedos
for his wedding instead of western suits, Cord had
told him it was Lori's idea. Not yet married to her,
Jed thought glumly, and already she was running the
show.

Impatient with his uncharitable thoughts, he
jammed his hands into the pockets of his pants and
just as quickly pulled them out again. He was being
ornery and he knew it. He liked Lori and he was
happy that Cord had found his special lady. It was
just that he was going to miss both Cord and Denver.

They'd traveled together for seven years, sharing
everything from a razor to a camper, and the road
was going to seem mighty empty now that two of
them had each found a wife.

Jed folded his arms across his chest, and felt the
tight pull of his rented jacket across his broad shoulders. He heard the quiet rustling of anticipation behind him as the familiar strains of the Wedding
March filled the room, and out of the corner of his

eye he saw Cord turn to watch his bride walk down the aisle.

Unable to resist a peek himself, Jed glanced over his shoulder. At the sight of Lori in a short white dress and veil he felt a fleeting moment of envy, and firmly squelched it. Denver's wedding was only three weeks away. This marriage thing was catching and Jed Cullen was the one member of the team who was not going to fall into that trap. Not that there was a woman out there who could haul him to the altar, in any case. Though the vision walking down the aisle in front of Lori could possibly get his attention for a few hours.

For a second or two he allowed himself to dwell pleasantly on the shapely curves visible beneath the pale blue dress the bridesmaid wore. Then he took a good look at her face.

For a moment he thought he was hallucinating. Then he blinked, and blinked again. He wasn't seeing things. It really was Kristi Ramsett tramping resolutely down the aisle toward him.

She sure as hell looked different. Her blond hair was smoothed up on top of her head, held there by a tiny crown of blue and white flowers. The blue, silky dress clung to her slim figure, then flared out just below her hips to end above her knees. Jed stared in amazement. Kristi Ramsett had legs. Good-looking legs at that. He couldn't ever remember a time when Kristi hadn't worn jeans and a cowboy shirt. Even when she went dancing.

She drew closer, and he noticed that she'd put makeup on her face. Not a lot, just enough to make

her eyes look bigger and her mouth softer. She had
the clearest blue eyes he'd ever seen. He'd never
noticed that before. Now that he came to think about
it, he'd never really paid attention to her mouth, either. He was noticing it now, all right.

She was smiling at him, and he swallowed as a
spark of awareness shot down his spine. He jerked
his head around and stared unseeingly in front of
him. He was vaguely aware of Cord stepping forward
with a radiant Lori at his side. He saw the priest
come down to greet them, and heard the pleasantly
low murmur of the words he spoke.

Jed tried to concentrate on the wedding, but his
mind kept wandering back to the woman who now
stood silently somewhere behind him.

He'd known Kristi for three years. Her father
owned the stockyards that supplied the horses and
cattle used in the rodeos on the western circuit. Now
and again Cord and Denver had teased him about the
way Kristi seemed to follow him around, always
popping up when he least expected it. Jed had firmly
put them straight on that score.

It wasn't as if he wasn't interested in women. He'd
spent some pretty memorable nights in the past with
a few of them. He just wasn't interested in anything
long-term. And Kristi definitely wasn't a one-night-
and-forget-it kind of woman. In fact, that was the
reason he'd always felt comfortable around her.
She'd never shown much interest in getting cozy
with a man.

Kristi Ramsett spent more of her time trying to
compete with the men she met. Jed had heard some-

where that she was trying to prove to her father that he hadn't missed out on anything by not having a son. There wasn't too much femininity about Kristi. She just wasn't Jed's kind of woman. So why the hell he kept wanting to turn around and take another look at her, he couldn't imagine.

Aware that the priest had paused in his sermon, Jed jerked his mind to attention. The priest was looking at him, as if he expected Jed to say something.

Jed saw Cord raise his eyebrows and mouth two words. *The ring.*

Jed started and dug his fingers into the narrow pocket of his vest. Damn. His big moment and he'd blown it. He found the small box and pulled it out of his pocket. In his haste to open it he fumbled and dropped the ring. It hit his boot and bounced off somewhere behind him.

Silently cursing, Jed twisted his head around to see where it had landed. What he saw was a clear view down the front of Kristi's dress when she stooped to pick up the gleaming circle of gold. Quickly she handed it to him, and he almost dropped it again while his mind grappled with the unexpected and inescapable fact that Kristi Ramsett also had breasts.

The priest cleared his throat, and Jed dragged his gaze away from Kristi's smirking face and faced front again. He handed the ring to the priest, who gave him a frown of disapproval before continuing with the service. Jed barely registered what happened after that. All he could think about was Kristi's transformation—and how soon he could look at her again and find out what else he'd missed.

* * *

Kristi, on the other hand, hung on every word of the service. It was the first time she'd ever been invited to be a bridesmaid, and she was determined to enjoy every second of it. That was proving to be more difficult than she'd anticipated, in view of the fact that her shoes were killing her. She'd never worn heels this high before, and the backs of her legs ached, while her toes felt as if they were being crushed like orange wedges in a juicer.

Thank heavens her father couldn't see her now. He probably wouldn't recognize her. She couldn't remember the last time she'd worn a dress. It had to be her high-school prom, and that dress had covered her ankles. This one made her feel as if she was wearing a shorty nightgown in public. Though it had been kind of satisfying to see the look on Jed Cullen's face when he'd caught sight of her. That alone was worth the agony.

She'd probably pay for that later, she thought gloomily, as she watched Cord and Lori each light a candle at the altar. Jed never missed an opportunity to tease her unmercifully, and he was bound to make the most of this one.

Her eyes misted up when she heard the priest announce that Cord and Lori were man and wife, and he could now kiss his bride. She refused to let a tear squeeze out, however. Crying was a sign of weakness, and Kristi Ramsett couldn't afford that luxury. She watched Cord kiss Lori, and felt a pang of envy. It must be wonderful to be in love with a man like that, and know that he loved you back. Lori was a lucky woman. She'd found her man and he obviously adored her.

Kristi sent a wistful glance at the back of Jed's head. She'd been waiting three years for Jed to take notice of her. All he did was treat her like a kid brother. Until today, that is.

She felt a little stirring of excitement. Maybe this would be the day he'd realize that there was more to Kristi Ramsett than spit and vinegar. Maybe for once he'd quit his teasing and treat her like a full-grown woman. After all, she was almost thirty years old. Over the hill, by some people's reckoning.

The object of her speculation suddenly spun around and faced her, and she realized that Lori and Cord were already halfway up the aisle. She took one look at Jed's square jaw and glinting gold eyes and immediately went on the defensive. "What are you grinning at, J. C.?" she muttered. "Never seen a freaking bridesmaid before?"

She was totally disconcerted when Jed, instead of giving her a smart answer as usual, let his gaze wander down the length of her body and back up again, making a big point of hovering at her breasts on the way. She was still trying to recover her breath when he gave her a slow grin, then offered her his arm to follow the newlyweds up the aisle.

With her hand resting in the crook of his elbow, she did her best to look as if she was used to walking in high heels and a skirt that kept flipping up with every step. She couldn't get over the way Jed looked in a tux, with his hair all slicked down. She rarely saw him without his hat pulled low on his forehead.

Without the hat's shadow, his light gold eyes seemed even more distinctive than usual…like the eyes of an exotic creature from the jungles of Africa.

Not that she'd ever been to Africa, she reminded herself, feeling somewhat self-conscious about her fanciful thoughts. But she'd seen eyes like that on animals in the zoo. Sometimes Jed reminded her of a wild animal…restless, somewhat primitive and more than a little dangerous. Yet other times he was like a playful puppy, teasing and fun-loving, practically begging someone to come play with him.

"You look about as comfortable as a fly in a shot of whiskey," he said, nodding at her feet.

"I could use a shot of whiskey right now," Kristi muttered, as they reached the end of the aisle.

"I wouldn't try it. I wouldn't want to see you tripping over those shoes and messing up that pretty face."

She shot him a suspicious look, but he'd turned away, apparently absorbed in ushering the guests out of the church and into their cars. She was left to wonder about that remark all the way back to the hotel where the reception was being held.

Jed did his best to forget the effect Kristi was having on him as he stood next to Cord and greeted the guests filing into the reception room. Kristi stood on the other side of the wedding couple, and out of sight—much to Jed's relief. He didn't need any more distractions.

It worried him that he found Kristi distracting enough to take his mind off his responsibilities. He kept assuring himself it was because she looked so different. He veered away from the word "attractive." He was not attracted to Kristi Ramsett. Not in any way, shape or form. Kristi was like a pesky, devious kid sister who occasionally got under his skin enough to make him want to pick her up and dump her into a tub of cold water.

Funny how the thought of that now seemed to curl his insides. She'd fight back, of course. If there was one thing Kristi had, it was spirit. He grinned at the thought of Kristi thrashing around in the water, mad as a rooster in a rainstorm, her clothes all wet and sticking to her body.

The heavyset woman he'd just greeted grinned back. "You look like you're having a good time, J. C. When's it going to be your turn?"

Jed stared at her, his mind still on the image of Kristi's clothes plastered to her wet body. It took a moment or two for him to recognized Grace, the rodeo secretary who handed him his winnings when he got lucky with his rides. When her question finally penetrated, it wiped the grin off his face. "I reckon hell's gonna have to freeze over before you see me in front of a priest."

She nodded cheerfully. "That's what I figured. Glad to see there's at least one of you boys with some sense in those thick skulls of yours. If everyone was like Cord and Denver, there'd be no more rodeo."

As always, Jed felt obliged to come to his friends' defense. "Hell, Grace, they're not giving up the rodeo. Denver's gonna open a rodeo school and train

future champs, and Cord's all set to produce his first
rodeo next year.''

Grace nodded. "So I hear. Won't be the same,
though, not seeing their butts in the saddle. It's good
to know you'll be back next year."

"I'm coming back a champ this time," Jed promised her. "So clear a spot on your wall to hang my
picture up with the rest of them."

Grace smiled as she moved on. "I'll do that."

Another woman paused in front of him, carrying
a tray loaded with brimming glasses of champagne.
"You'd better grab one," Cord said at his elbow.
"You have to give the speech, remember?"

Jed groaned. "How could I forget? You made me
rehearse it enough times to fill the pages of a whole
set of encyclopedias."

Cord grinned. "Hope you can remember it all."
He turned to grasp his new wife by the arm. "Let's
go, Mrs. McVane. It's time to position ourselves in
front of the cake."

Lori laughed up at him, and Jed followed them
over to a long table, where he picked up a fork and
chimed his glass. He had to repeat the sound several
times before he had everyone's attention. He cleared
his throat, and met Kristi's clear blue gaze across the
room. Hastily he focused on a small group of men
standing next to her. "Ladies and gentlemen," he
began, "I just want to say..." For a moment he
couldn't remember what he wanted to say. Damn
Kristi. And damn the slinky dress that matched her
eyes.

Aware of everyone's gaze riveted on him, he

cleared his throat again, and felt a cluster of sweat beads forming on his forehead. "It isn't just anyone who can capture the heart of a rodeo man," he began, "it takes someone pretty special...."

He relaxed as the well-rehearsed speech came back to him. He got through it without a hitch, his gaze resting on anyone who wasn't Kristi Ramsett. Finally, with a deep sense of relief, he held up his glass. "I reckon everyone will want to join me in wishing the happy couple a long life of happiness and good health. To our real good friends, Cord and Lori McVane."

As his audience raised their glasses, Jed tipped his head back and poured the entire glass of champagne down his throat. He managed to down another one while Cord and Lori fed each other pieces of wedding cake. When the band struck up a slow waltz, signaling the happy couple to the dance floor, he finished off a third glass.

He was reaching for his fourth when Denver's deep voice said dryly from behind him, "You don't have to drink champagne. There's plenty of beer at the bar over there."

"I like champagne," Jed said defiantly. Right then he would have drunk just about anything to quell the jitters that kept invading his stomach. He watched Cord relinquish his bride to the arms of her father. "Nice wedding," he added.

"Yep. Reckon it's good practice for mine." He glanced at Jed. "Now if we can just get you to the altar..."

Jed gave his head an emphatic shake. "No, sir. Not me. Not nohow."

"Thought you wanted to take a bride back to Promise with you," Denver said, accepting a piece of cake from a smiling young woman.

"A *pretend* bride," Jed corrected. "All I want to do is put on a show for a few people, not ruin my life."

"The people in your hometown must get impressed real easy if that's all it takes."

Jed grunted. "You know it's more than that. I'm figuring on winning the all-around championship buckle the day after tomorrow. When I take that back to Promise, Arizona, which just happens to be the most rodeo-loving town in the West, they'll all sit up and take notice. If that don't earn me some respect, I reckon nothing will."

"You got to win it first, as I keep reminding you," Denver said amiably. "There's a few of us here who figure we can beat you."

"I'm up pretty high in the standings." Jed shook his head at the woman who offered him a piece of cake. "I got as good a chance as any of them, I reckon."

"What if you do win it? Are you still gonna go looking for a pretend bride?"

Jed shrugged. "I guess I'll have to give up on that idea. I was figuring on finding one of them elegant, sophisticated women who knows how to dress and talk real fancy. Haven't run into too many like that, though."

"I reckon you ought to take a piece of that cake,"

Denver said solemnly. "You've got a lot of wishing to do, and you're gonna need some help."

Jed frowned. "What's that got to do with cake?"

"Wishes on wedding cake always come true. Didn't you know that?"

Jed narrowed his eyes. "I know when you're joshing me, that's for sure."

"Now why would I do that, pardner? All you're planning on doing is beat out fourteen hot-riding cowboys to win the most prestigious, all important buckle in rodeo, then find yourself a rich society dame to take back to Promise, Arizona to impress some small-town folks. Now why in tarnation would I find a joke in that?"

Jed swallowed his anger. He'd done more than his share of joking in the past, and he couldn't expect Denver to understand. He'd never told him or Cord the whole story. Put in so many words like that, his plans did sound pretty far-fetched. "She doesn't have to be rich," he said lightly. "Just look like she's got money. Anyway, I guess I'll have to forget that part of it. One thing I can promise you, though. I am gonna win that buckle."

"Well, since I'm not competing this year, you might have a chance, at that." Denver slapped his friend on the shoulder. "I'll wish you luck with that one, J. C."

"And may the best man win." Cord said, appearing at Jed's side. "Now will you do me a favor?"

"Sure," Jed said eagerly. "Just name it, pardner."

Cord nodded his head at the dance floor behind Jed. "It's sort of traditional that the best man dance with the chief bridesmaid. I know it would make Lori happy if you took a turn or two around the floor with Kristi. She's real set on traditions.''

Jed swallowed, and managed a weak grin. "Tell Mrs. McVane it'll be a pleasure. As long as I get to dance with *her* later.''

Cord pretended to think about it. "I guess I can trust her with you for one dance,'' he said finally.

"Come to think of it,'' Jed stroked his chin with his fingers, "I don't suppose you'd lend me your wife for a couple of weeks in Promise, Arizona?''

Cord gave him a lazy smile. "Sorry, pardner. I've got plans for that little lady that are gonna keep her pretty busy for a while.''

Jed looked at Denver.

"Forget it.'' Denver gave him a mock scowl. "Go find your own class act.''

"In that case,'' Jed glanced over his shoulder to where Kristi stood talking to Grace, "I guess I'll take my chances with the chief bridesmaid.''

Kristi saw him ambling across the floor toward her and felt her heart skip a beat. She knew she was supposed to dance with the best man, but in all the time Kristi had known Jed, she'd never seen him on the dance floor. She was afraid to hope that he was actually coming to ask her to join him out there.

At the same time, she wasn't sure she wanted to dance. Her feet hurt so bad she could hardly stand up on the dumb heels. She just couldn't imagine dancing on the damn things. Especially with Jed Cullen.

One of the reasons Kristi had managed to reach

the ripe old age of thirty without getting hitched was that she'd never met a man she could trust. Except for maybe the man striding across the floor toward her and his two travel partners.

All three men were respected around the circuit, and now both Cord and Denver had found someone to share their lives. As for Jed Cullen, well, he was a lot of things, and sometimes he drove her nuts with his teasing, but she'd never heard anyone say a bad word against him.

His biggest problem was that he never took anything seriously, except for the rodeo. No one was more serious about winning the championship than Jed Cullen. It was his life's ambition, which was probably why he never had time for anything else. Including her, Kristi thought dismally.

She watched him warily as he paused in front of her and she braced to counter one of his smart remarks. She'd told herself, many times, that Jed wouldn't bother razzing her if he didn't like her. But sometimes his teasing hurt, though he'd probably be real upset if he knew that. She couldn't let him know that, of course. She could never let him find out that she dreamed about him at night, and fantasized about him when she was feeling lonely. If he ever discovered that, he'd stay clear out of her way, and she'd miss his teasing. Even if it did hurt sometimes.

"I figure there must be a long line of cowboys waiting to dance with you," he said, as he held out his hand, "so I thought I'd stake my claim before I have to fight them all off."

Kristi wrinkled her nose at him. "Yeah, I noticed they were all panting to get over here."

"I'm not kidding." He gestured with his head in the direction of the bar. "There's at least three of them arguing over who gets to ask you first." His gaze traveled down her body and back up. "Can't say I blame them, the way you look."

Kristi felt her breath stick in her throat. Was he kidding or not? Her heartbeat quickened as she met his gaze, and for once she couldn't think of an answer.

"Are you gonna take my hand or do I have to drag you on the floor?"

She stared at his outstretched hand as if it might suddenly burst into flame, then silently cursed herself for being such a wimp. Doing her best to look unconcerned, she put her hand in his.

His fingers felt warm and strong when he clasped hers, and she felt the heat of his touch all the way up her arm. He started out onto the floor and she followed him, stumbling for a moment on the pesky heel of her shoe.

He looked back at her with a look of concern on his face. "You okay?"

She nodded, gritting her teeth in an effort to walk naturally. Her knees felt shaky, and she put it down to the strain of standing on the heels for so long.

Jed paused, and turned to face her. Still holding her fingers tight in his, he snaked his other hand around her back and pulled her closer to him. She bumped against him and muttered, "Sorry."

"Hell, I'm not." He grinned down at her. "You can bump into me any old time."

She felt heat spreading across her cheeks and shifted her gaze to where several cowboys lounged against the bar. At least three of them *were* watching her with Jed, she noticed. Probably taking bets on how long he'd last before taking off to look for someone a little more his style.

"Nice dress," Jed commented, putting his mouth so close to her ear she could feel his warm breath.

She jumped, and stumbled again on her heels.

His arm tightened around her. "How come you're so jumpy?"

She mumbled something about not being a very good dancer.

"Nor am I. So why don't we just stand here and sway to the music? You can do that, can't you?"

She pulled back to give him an accusing look. "Are you making fun of me?"

His eyes widened, and as always when she saw the gleam of mischief in his glittering golden gaze, she felt a thrill chase up her spine.

"Hell, no," he said huskily. "Now why would I make fun of one of the prettiest women in the room? You don't look a bit like good ol' Kristi. What I'd like to know is where you've been hiding that body of yours all this time."

Oh, God, she thought frantically. He had noticed. Now what did she do? She felt awkward, unsure of herself. His teasing, even when it bordered on insults, she knew how to deal with. She'd always managed to have a smart answer to come back at him. But this was different. This was something she'd fantasized about for years, but now that it was actually happening, she didn't know how to handle it. She couldn't think of one clever thing to say.

"It's been there all the time," she said tartly, and immediately wished she'd kept her mouth shut.

"You're kidding." Jed smiled at her. "Who would have thought that under those big ol' western shirts and baggy jeans you were hiding such awesome equipment."

His words had slurred just a little, and she frowned as the suspicion dawned. "Have you been drinking?"

He nodded happily. "Champagne. Lots of good bubbly."

"So that's it."

She tried to pull out of his arms but he held her fast. "Hey, wait a minute. I haven't had that much. Not enough that I can't recognize a beautiful woman when I hold one."

"What'd you do? Drink the whole bottle?"

He sighed. "What do I have to do to convince you? Kiss you?"

The thought was so unnerving she stumbled again, and this time almost fell.

Jed grabbed hold of her and she slammed hard against his chest. For a second or two the major portion of her anatomy was pasted to his, and all the breath rushed out of her lungs. Her skin seemed to frizzle with excitement. In that moment she felt hot, then cold, then hot again. She wanted to stay there forever, jammed against the hard contours of his body, with the musky fragrance of his cologne making her head swim.

For a moment the impact of Kristi's soft body stunned Jed. All the time he'd been dancing with her he'd been asking himself how come he'd never noticed before the way Kristi's mouth curved in hot invitation, or the dimple that appeared at the base of her right cheek when she smiled. Now he was noticing a whole lot more. The way her body fitted snugly against his, for instance, and how she went in and out at all the right places.

The knot of hair on top of her head brushed his cheek, and he felt an almost irresistible urge to pull it loose from its bonds and let it fall free. He couldn't remember seeing Kristi wear her hair loose, and he wanted to see it now in the worst way. She smelled good, too, like a bed of roses after a dawn shower. He drew in a long breath of her, and felt giddy.

"Reckon it's my turn to dance with the bridesmaid," someone said behind him.

Instinctively he tightened his arms around his dance partner. He wanted to tell whoever it was to go away. He hadn't expected this dance with Kristi to be so much fun. This was a side of her he'd never seen...and he liked it. He liked it a lot.

"Hey, pardner," the voice behind him insisted, "you're supposed to ask the bride for a dance."

Annoyed by the intrusion, Jed turned his head.

Amusement flickered in Cord's black gaze as he murmured, "You planning on keeping her all to yourself all night, pardner?"

It was as if a light clicked on in Jed's brain. What the hell was he doing, making a move on Kristi Ramsett? He dropped his arms and backed away from her as if she'd suddenly developed an infectious disease. "Just doing my duty," he said lightly. "She's all yours."

He saw Kristi's smile fade, and didn't dare analyze the reason. Surely she hadn't taken him seriously? Worried now, he shot across the room and grabbed a startled Lori by the hand. "My turn to dance with the bride," he announced, and whisked her onto the floor a little too fast for the slow beat that the band strummed out.

Anxious to prove that his hot moment with Kristi had been just his normal way of dancing, he wrapped his arms around Lori and began moving rapidly around the outer edge of the dancers. After a moment or two Lori asked breathlessly, "Are we winning?"

He looked down at her with a frown. "Winning?"

"Well, the way we're speeding around, I thought we might be in some sort of race."

He gave her a sheepish grin. "Sorry. I never did take much to dancing. Takes too long to get where you're going."

Lori sent a significant glance over to where Kristi was dancing with Cord. "I guess the trip depends on who's traveling with you."

Jed frowned. He wasn't too sure what Lori meant by that, but he didn't think he cared for the way she said it. Deciding that the safest way to deal with a barbed comment like that was to ignore it, he deftly changed the subject by asking Lori where she and Cord planned to spend their honeymoon.

He was intrigued to find out they were going to spend the week after the finals at Cord's rustic cabin in the mountains. He would have bet an even buck that Lori would want to go to some place fancy like Paris, or Rome. Just went to prove what he'd always known. Women were damned tough to figure out.

He deliberately kept his gaze off Kristi for the rest of the evening. He didn't know what had gotten into him when he'd danced with her, and he didn't want to know. He put the entire blame for the way he'd been feeling on the champagne. He just wasn't used to drinking bubbly, and by golly, that stuff could make a man think a rhinoceros was attractive.

He'd feel a lot better after a good night's sleep, he promised himself as he drove the truck back to the camper. Everything would be back to normal by then. In any case, right now he had too much to think about to waste time worrying about his reaction to Kristi Ramsett. The national finals were only two days away, and he'd have his work cut out to win those buckles. He had to win the saddle-bronc buckle, in order to have a chance at the all-around. And this time he was bound and determined he was not going to come away without it.

Thinking about the finals sobered him up as nothing else could have done, and by the time he fell into bed his mind was clear as a mountain spring. This was the year he was going take the championship home to Promise. He'd waited a long time. Too long.

He had to get back there before the folks in town forgot who he was.

He'd left his hometown sixteen years ago under a murky cloud of suspicion and fear. There were a lot of folks still there who wouldn't be happy to see him back. Not at first, anyway. But once they found out he was the world's best rodeo cowboy, they'd soon change their tune.

Respect, that's all he wanted. They owed him that much. They'd judged him all those years ago, and they'd been wrong. The championship would help him go back and prove it. That, and the little visit from a good friend a while back. What Luke Tucker had given him could help a lot.

Jed sighed, and rolled onto his back, staring up at the dark ceiling. If only he'd managed the second part of the plan, he'd feel a lot more confident about its success. Sarah's rejection had hurt him more than anything else back then. He'd have given anything for the opportunity to go home again with a high-society wife on his arm. Among other things, he needed to show the town that he didn't need any of them, and especially not Sarah Hammond, to make him a success.

But since that didn't look too possible now, the championship would have to do. All he had to do was win it. That buckle had his name on it already. He could just see it gleaming on his belt.

He closed his eyes and concentrated on his goal. He had to win it this year. He was taking that damn buckle back to Promise and he was going to shove it down their throats...and he wasn't about to let anything or anyone stop him.

Chapter 2

Kristi awoke on the last day of the finals with a sense of excited anticipation. She always looked forward to the championship rodeo, but this one had been special so far…and the last day promised to be even more spectacular.

Cord had lost three of his nine rounds so far, effectively eliminating him from the all-around race. Jed had hung in there and was still in contention for the saddle-bronc championship.

It had been a grueling nine days, and Kristi had sat through every one of them cheering in the stands with April and Lori. It had always been thrilling to watch Jed battle his way through the rounds, but never more than this year. This year had been different. She hadn't been able to look at him over the past two days without remembering the approval in his eyes and his suggestive comments when he'd danced with her on the day of Cord's wedding.

She hadn't had a chance to talk to him for more than a few minutes at a time since then, and never alone. He'd treated her as he'd always done. He'd acted as if those magical moments on the dance floor had never happened. But Kristi had the memories to hold in her heart and she refused to let them go. She relived them over and over, seeing again the golden glint of his eyes, the sexy tilt of his mouth when he smiled, the husky drawl that could make her knees weak every time he spoke to her.

Now he had one more round to go in the finals. He was in second place in the all-around standings by a substantial amount, and his chances for winning the prestigious buckle didn't look good. Even if he won the saddle-bronc round, it still wouldn't give him enough to catch up with the leader, a fiery-eyed, dark-haired cowboy by the name of Clint Becker.

Kristi knew Jed would be bitterly disappointed to lose the championship. He'd set so much store on winning that buckle and taking it back to Arizona, though she never could understand why it was so important to him.

All Clint had to do was win his round today, and the gold buckle would be his. Everyone said that Clint was a surefire winner of the top prize, and Kristi wanted to be there to offer her support when Jed left the arena. She was reasonably sure that he was going to win the saddle-bronc championship, and she just hoped that would be enough. In any case, she was determined to be there, to let him know that she was ready to lend a sympathetic ear if he wanted to pour out his troubles. She was hoping with all her heart that he'd take her up on the offer.

The urgent ring of her cell phone jolted her out of her contemplation. She stretched out a hand to retrieve it from the built-in shelf next to her bed.

"I thought I might have missed you," her father said in his familiar deep baritone. "How are the finals going?"

"Great." She paused, trying to get the accusation out of her voice before adding, "Too bad you couldn't make it. Everyone's been asking about you."

"I know, I should have come. But things are so hectic here...the end of the season is always a mess...you should know that."

"That's what managers are for. Why can't Ted handle things for a while?"

There was a pause, while her heart skipped a beat. Something was wrong. She waited, barely breathing, for him to continue.

"Ted's not with us anymore," her father said at last.

"What happened?"

"We had a little disagreement. Nothing much, but he used it for an excuse to quit."

Kristi held her breath. Could this be the moment she'd been waiting for the past twelve long years? Could her father actually be considering her for his new manager? After all this time, had he finally realized that she was capable of running Ramsett Stockyards as well as any man...if not better? She made an effort to reveal none of her wishful thinking when she answered him. "So, what are you going to do now?"

"Kristi..."

She closed her eyes and prayed.

"I've decided to sell the stockyards."

She snapped her eyes open, her jaw dropping in shocked disbelief. "You've *what?*"

"I figured you'd be upset, but I've been thinking about it for some time. I think it's the right thing to do. This thing with Ted has just about clinched it. I'm tired, and I want to spend some time traveling and catching up on all the things I've missed these past years. I've made my decision, and I really don't want to argue about it. I'm putting the business on the market tomorrow."

"Tomorrow?" She choked on the word, then drew a deep breath. She would not cry. She hadn't cried since the day her mother died, twenty-five years ago, and she wasn't about to start now.

"I know it's a shock," Paul Ramsett said, sounding more uncomfortable than she ever remembered him being, "but you'll soon get used to the idea. After all, we both knew I couldn't go on running the place for ever."

No, she thought bitterly, *but I could have run it. Didn't you ever think of that?* There was no point in arguing with him. If there was one area where Paul Ramsett was consistent it was in his decisions. If he hadn't realized her capabilities by now, he never would.

Swallowing her resentment, she said carefully, "I

have to run along. The finals will be starting in an hour and I want to watch Jed Cullen go for the saddle-bronc race. I'll try to stop by over Christmas.''

"Stop by? I thought you were going to spend the whole weekend with me.''

She hardened her heart against the hurt in his voice. "Well, something came up.''

"I see." Again he paused. "Does this have anything to do with my decision to sell?"

She lied. She wasn't about to let him know how much he'd hurt her. "No, of course not. I promise I'll make it for an hour or two over the holidays.''

"Well, I reckon that will have to do. I'll look forward to seeing you.''

She hung up, swallowing hard against the lump in her throat. Ever since graduation she'd worked for her father, busting her butt to prove to him she could handle anything a man could handle. Paul Ramsett had made no secret of the fact that his biggest regret in life was not having sons to carry on the family business.

Kristi had sworn to show him she was as good as any son, and perfectly capable of managing the Ramsett Stockyards. She'd worked her heart out, often to the point of exhaustion, and had won the respect of every man she'd worked with, except for her father.

And now this. The ultimate betrayal. He was selling out without even considering the fact that he had a daughter who not only had the experience and skills to run the business but had earned the right to do so. It just wasn't fair. And feeling the way she did, she couldn't see how she was going to spend the Christmas holidays with her father, trying to pretend it didn't matter.

She tried to push her dejection aside as she joined the crowds streaming into the vast Thomas and Mack Center. When she reached her row, Lori and April were already there, with Denver seated between them. Kristi edged past a row of knees to reach her seat, and sat down with a sigh.

"I thought you were going to miss the opening ceremonies," Lori said, giving her a smile. "You must have slept late."

Kristi shook her head. "I got a phone call from my father."

Lori's gaze sharpened. "Everything all right?"

Kristi smiled ruefully. She and Lori had shared the camper for a while earlier that year, and the two of them had become pretty close. She might have known she couldn't hide her disappointment from her friend. "As a matter of fact, he had some bad news. He's putting the stockyards up for sale."

Lori's dark eyes filled with sympathy. "Oh, Kristi, I'm so sorry. I know how much you wanted to take over the business."

Kristi looked gloomily around at the crowds seated in the stands. "All these years. All for nothing. I might just as well have done something else with my life. In fact, that's just what I'm going to do." She drew an unsteady breath as the conviction took shape in her mind. "I'm going to quit rodeo and do something else entirely."

Lori frowned. "Are you sure? The rodeo has been

your life. Do you have any idea what you want to
do?''

"Not really. I just know I want to get out of all
this.'' She waved a hand at the empty arena. "It's
about time I found out what else I can do, besides
take care of rodeo stock.''

April chose that moment to lean forward and send
her a wave. "It's Jed's big day,'' she called out. "He
should win the saddle-bronc buckle.''

Kristi nodded. "I hope so.''

"Cord's just about given up on winning his race,''
Lori said, peering down at the arena as music blared
from the speakers. "I think they've both given up on
the all-around.''

Within moments, the rodeo began and they all
waited eagerly to see Cord compete in the bareback
competition. He rode well, won his round and managed to place second overall, much to Lori's delight.
She'd worried that he might not place at all.

Denver watched the opening of the bull-riding
event with a gloomy expression on his face. He
should have been down there competing, but a bad
fall from a belligerent bull had injured his back, and
now Denver would never ride again.

This was Cord's last ride, Kristi remembered suddenly. She leaned toward Lori, asking, "How does
Cord feel about giving up the rodeo?''

Lori raised her eyebrows and shrugged. "He says
he won't miss having his bones jolted around, or being thrown to the ground and trampled on. And he's
really not giving up the rodeo, just changing his part
in it. I think he's looking forward to going into the

production side. I never did like the idea of him risking life and limb out there. And now he has good reason to take better care of himself.''

She patted her stomach, and Kristi grinned. Lori was three months pregnant with Cord's baby, and Cord hadn't stopped talking about it since the wedding. She turned her attention back to the arena, where Clint Becker sat in the chutes, waiting to take his turn on the bull.

The chunky cowboy gave a sharp nod of his head and the gate slammed open. The massive bull thundered out into the ring, snorting and twisting his body in a furious effort to rid himself of the irritating weight on his back. Clint rose and fell with the enraged animal, his lithe body whipped around like a reed in the summer wind.

It happened so quickly Kristi missed the moment when Clint lost his balance. The next thing she knew, a cry of dismay rippled through the audience, while the clowns drew the bull away from the fallen cowboy. Kristi watched him scramble to his feet and limp for the fence amid sympathetic applause from the spectators.

''That will give Jed a shot at the all-around,'' Denver commented, raising his voice over the announcer.

Kristi's pulse leapt. She wanted so much for Jed to win, mostly because he wanted it so badly himself. Ever since she'd known him he'd talked about winning the championship. Now he had his chance.

She waited impatiently through the next two rounds, until at last the saddle-bronc competition was announced. Both Lori and April leaned forward with expectant expressions on their faces, while Denver stared stoically at the chutes. What was it with rodeo cowboys, Kristi wondered, that they rarely showed any emotion in tense moments?

She soon forgot about Denver when she saw the first rider thrown from his horse. There were only three real contenders for the saddle-bronc race—Jed, and two others. The first rider, a young cowboy with flaming red hair, finished his ride with seventy-nine points. The second cowboy touched the flank of his horse with his free hand, and was disqualified. All Jed had to do was beat the seventy-nine put up by the redhead.

Kristi's chest ached with holding her breath. She could feel her heart thumping madly as she watched Jed climb up onto the chute. It wasn't just a matter of staying on. Jed had to be sure his horse was marked out, hold his spurs set above the horse's shoulders and keep them there until the horse's front feet hit the ground after the initial jump. If Jed let his feet drop below the mark, he'd be disqualified.

He'd receive points for his spurring and skill in controlling the animal. The horse earned points for bucking performance. If Jed had drawn a quieter horse, he could lose points.

Kristi's gaze remained fixed on Jed as he poised himself above the horse, then lowered himself onto the animal's back. The gate opened, and he was through. The crowd murmured as the duel began, man against beast, skill against brute strength. In spite of the violent contortions of the horse, Jed managed to look graceful as he synchronized his movements with that of the plunging animal.

The seconds ticked by, but to Kristi they seemed interminable. When the buzzer sounded, the echo of it broke the silence of the crowd in the stands. Jed dropped from the horse and sprinted for the fence, and the harsh voice of the announcer was almost drowned out by the applause. Kristi heard it, though. Jed had scored eighty-four points, enough to give him the saddle-bronc championship. The earnings from the win was just enough to give him the all-around title. He had earned more than any other cowboy on the circuit that season. Jed had finally realized his dream.

It wasn't until the close of the competition that Jed allowed himself to believe that the championship buckle was his. He hadn't expected to win. He'd accepted the news that he'd won the saddle-bronc buckle in a daze, aware that without that the bigger prize would have been out of his grasp. But now there he was, listening to the thunderous applause that signaled the end of the finals, with the knowledge that he was the all-around champion. The best of the best.

This was what he'd been waiting for, ever since he'd left his hometown behind. He felt pride in what he'd achieved, thrilled to think he'd beaten out every other cowboy on the circuit. The best of the best. But when it came right down to it, the title meant different things to different people. To Jed Cullen it meant only one thing, and the realization hit him like a sledgehammer. He had done what he'd set out to do sixteen years ago. Now he could go back to Promise, Arizona and give them a champion.

He didn't notice Denver and Cord waiting for him in the dusty passageway behind the chutes until he was almost on top of them. He grinned and held up his hand, accepting their bone-jarring backslapping with good humor. Outside in the cold desert air, a small group of people waited to congratulate him. The next few minutes passed in a hazy blur of confusion.

He saw April and gave her a bear hug. With Lori he was a little more careful, aware of the tiny life forming in her belly. Kristi was there, too, smiling and holding out her arms for a hug. He held her briefly, then let her go, already turning to answer someone else's eager question.

He didn't remember afterward what was said or by whom. All he could think about was how soon he could be on the road to Promise. He'd have to rent a car, find somewhere to leave the camper, and take care of a number of things before he'd be ready to leave. Now that he'd made up his mind, he was anxious to be on the way. A day or two at the most, and he'd be going home.

When Cord reminded him that they'd all be at the awards banquet the next night to see him accept his buckles, some of his euphoria faded. This would probably be one of the last times they would all be together. That depressed him. It had been a great seven years.

But now it was over, and time to move on. He

didn't know what kind of reception awaited him in Promise, but he was anxious to find out. This was something he had to do before he could get on with the rest of his life. He had to set the record straight, somehow. They wouldn't listen to him before, because back then he'd been a nobody. A kid from the wrong side of the tracks. But now it was different. Now he had the title, and maybe the key to clearing his name as well.

Kristi spent the next morning alternating between dejection and anticipation. Her father's decision to sell the stockyards still weighed heavily on her mind, but uppermost was the coming celebration that evening. It would be the first chance she'd had since the wedding to talk to Jed, and she was determined to make the most of it.

Only one thought marred her excitement. Jed's attitude toward her the night before had shown a marked difference from the night of the wedding. True, he'd been drinking champagne that night, but she'd been in bars with him before and he'd never acted like that.

Then again, last night he'd been surrounded by people all talking to him at once, and hadn't had a chance to say anything. Still, his casual indifference to her hug had stung, and she wasn't sure how to take it.

It had to be the dress, she thought, as she studied her meager wardrobe that afternoon. The wedding was the first time he'd seen her in a dress. That was why he'd paid so much attention to her. If she hoped to get his attention tonight, she had better find herself another one, since she could hardly turn up in her bridesmaid dress again.

Luckily her bank balance was in pretty good shape, considering it was the holiday season. She could afford to splurge out on a decent dress for her last night with the boys. Excited now at the thought, she called a cab, then charged out of the camper to wait for it.

She spent a couple of hours choosing just the right dress for the banquet. Not too flashy, but enough to grab attention. She finally settled on a slinky black number that was deceptively demure with its high neckline in front, but bared her shoulders and laced halfway down her back. The hem halted provocatively above her knees, and she found a pair of black sandals with heels a little more comfortable than the stilts she'd worn at the wedding.

Satisfied with her purchases, she rushed home again to prepare for the banquet. Tonight she would see Jed's dream come true, and just maybe, one of hers as well.

''Well, pardner, this is your big night,'' Cord said, handing Jed a mug of beer. ''I reckon Denver and I have to pay up on our bet now.''

Jed shook his head. ''Forget it. Getting that buckle in my hot little hand is all I really care about. The bet was off when Denver messed up his back.''

Cord grinned. ''That's pretty generous of you, pardner.''

''I can afford to be generous, seeing as how I made

more'n anybody on the circuit this year.'' Jed took a swig of his beer and glanced across the crowded room to where Lori sat with Denver and April. "How's married life suiting you, anyway?"

"Better than I ever imagined." He slapped Jed on the back, slopping some of the beer out of Jed's glass. "You should try it sometime. You can sure afford it now that you've got all that money."

Jed snorted. "Take more than money to make me want to tie myself down to one woman. Nothing but trouble, that's—'' He broke off, his words freezing in his throat. The woman walking across the floor to his partners' table looked real familiar...at least the way she walked reminded him of someone. No, it couldn't be.

But it was. Kristi Ramsett. Damn, that woman had a way of surprising him lately.

"Something wrong?"

Cord's dry tone broke into his thoughts, and he hastily shifted his gaze back to his friend. "No...I just thought...never mind."

Cord nodded solemnly. "Time we went back to the table, I reckon. I see Kristi's arrived."

"She has?" His voice broke, and he cleared his throat. "I didn't notice."

"Yeah, and I'm the president of the United States." Cord's grin widened. "Come on, take that stupefied look off your face and let's get back to the women."

Jed wasn't at all sure he wanted to go back to the table. He couldn't forget what the champagne had done to him the last time he'd seen Kristi all fancied up, and he wasn't too confident it wouldn't happen again. He had to hand it to her, when she took the trouble to dress up like that, it sure paid off. Kristi Ramsett was a good-looking woman, and he couldn't help noticing there was more than one man sending hopeful glances her way.

Deciding that he might as well enjoy the evening, he followed Cord back to the little group. Kristi's smile dazzled him, and he muttered a vague greeting before seating himself on the opposite side of the table from where she sat.

"It's nice that you could all come to see me get my buckle," Jed said, hoping to break the sudden tension that seemed to hover over them all. Or maybe it was just him feeling as if he were walking on a bed of stinging nettles.

"Are you still planning on going back to your hometown, Jed?" April asked.

"Yep." Jed looked down at the beer clasped between his hands. "I reckon it's time to show those people in Promise, Arizona what a real champion looks like. They've been waiting for one for a long time."

"I hope it all turns out the way you want," Cord said quietly.

Jed exchanged a quick glance with him. "Thanks. So do I." He had never told anyone the whole story of what happened back there. But Cord was smart enough to figure out the stakes were high, and he appreciated his friend's good wishes.

"Too bad you didn't find a wife to take back," Denver said lazily, as he wound an arm around

April's shoulders. "I reckon you'll have to make do with a fancy car and that gold buckle on your belt, after all."

Jed felt Kristi's gaze move over his face, but when he glanced at her she seemed to be interested in something Lori was saying to her. He felt relieved. He didn't want her getting the wrong idea, just because he found her attractive when she was all prettied up.

Trying to distract himself from thoughts of Kristi, Jed concentrated instead on the meal that was now being served. He watched the waiters scurrying back and forth, he ordered a single-malt Scotch, he ate his chicken and ribs and the chocolate soufflé, and now and again he sent sidelong glances across the table at Kristi when he figured she wasn't noticing.

He wasn't exactly sure when the idea formed in his mind. Maybe it was after the Scotch or the second beer. Maybe it was when he returned to the table after being presented with his gold buckle and she congratulated him. Or just maybe the idea had been in his head all the time and he'd refused to consider it before.

Whenever it had happened, the idea was there now, burning in his brain with an urgency he couldn't ignore. There was only one way he was going to deal with its persistence. Sending up a silent prayer that what he was about to do wouldn't turn out to be the biggest mistake of his life, he got to his feet. He wasn't used to asking women to dance. Usually he avoided the dance floor at all costs, wary of being that close to a woman and on display.

It had seemed much easier to ask Kristi at the wedding. For some reason, the words seemed to be stuck in his throat now. It didn't help when she turned her clear blue gaze on him with a look of expectation on her face. Cord chose that moment to finish what he was saying and the entire group at the table fell silent.

Jed cleared his throat and did his best to sound casual. "I feel like some exercise. How about it, Kristi? Want to take a turn around the floor?"

She hesitated, and for an awful moment he thought she was going to refuse, but then she pushed her chair back. "Sure, why not."

She'd sounded even more indifferent than he had, and he followed her onto the floor with a small frown. What he was going to ask her was probably the most important thing he'd ever asked of anyone. It hadn't occurred to him that she might actually turn him down. Now that he'd made up his mind, he couldn't bear the thought of being denied the chance to do what he'd dreamed of doing for so long.

The uncertainty of the outcome made him nervous, and he trod on her toes twice before she said impatiently, "Why the heck did you ask me to dance if you're not going to enjoy it?"

Guiltily he pinned a smile on his face. "Who says I'm not enjoying it?"

"That scowl on your face would frighten off a mad bull, and you're stomping so hard on my feet I'll be lucky to be walking tomorrow."

"Well, keep your pesky feet out of my way." He looked down at her, concentrating on her face for the

first time. She'd put makeup on again. He couldn't
get over how a dab of powder here and there could
make her look so damn good. He tripped on her foot
again, and cursed himself for his clumsiness. "Sorry.
I reckon I need to keep my mind on my feet."

She smiled, and immediately he felt the warmth
of it spreading across his chest. "I reckon you have
reason to be woolgathering at that. It isn't every day
a man gets to win the World All-Around buckle.
Now you can go back to your hometown just like
you wanted to, as the world champion."

He swallowed. She'd given him the opening he
needed, but now he wasn't so sure he wanted to pur-
sue it. He had to be crazy thinking she'd go for it. It
was a big thing he was asking.

When he looked at her again he realized she was
staring at him with a puzzled expression on her face.
"What's wrong, Jed?" she asked softly. "Why don't
you tell me what's eating at you?"

For an instant the usual pat phrase hovered on his
lips, then he decided to go for broke. Even so, he
felt a moment of panic as he said, "I'm looking for
someone to go back to Promise with me and pretend
to be my wife."

His statement didn't have the effect he expected.
He wasn't sure what he'd expected, but it sure wasn't
the calm way Kristi answered him.

"So I heard."

Obviously she didn't understand. He tried again.
"I was wondering if you'd take on the job. I'll pay
all your expenses, and you get to keep anything I
give you while you're acting as my wife."

This time her eyes widened in disbelief. "Me?"

He shrugged. "It was just an idea."

"But Cord said you were looking for someone rich and sophisticated. This is me, remember? Good old Kristi."

He shook his head. "You don't have to *be* rich, you just have to look it." He held her away from him for a moment and ran his gaze up and down her slender figure. "You look good in a dress, and as long as you don't tell anyone you work for the rodeo, and you don't cuss anyone out, you could pass easy for one of those rich society women."

She stared at him for so long he began to get worried. Ever since he'd known Kristi he'd had fun teasing her. Sometimes she took it well, sometimes she didn't. She had a look on her face now that suggested she wasn't too thrilled with his idea. His spirits sank. He might have known she wouldn't go for it. He just hoped she wasn't going to cuss him out in the middle of the dance floor and embarrass him.

He was all set to tell her to forget he ever asked, when she said, "I'd like to think about it."

He shut his mouth with a snap. It wasn't much, but there was still hope. As he led her off the dance floor he couldn't believe how hard he was hoping she'd agree to his suggestion. What worried him was that he wasn't sure just how much that had to do with his wanting to impress the townsfolk of Promise, and exactly how much it had to do with the fact that he couldn't take his eyes off the smooth expanse of bare flesh beneath the lacing on her dress.

* * *

Kristi's mind was in a whirl as she took her seat at the table. She couldn't believe that Jed had asked her to go back to Promise with him. She'd almost told him to go to hell when he'd looked her over as if she were a prize heifer. Something had stopped her. There had been something in his eyes when he'd mentioned taking a wife back with him. She wasn't sure what it was, but she was pretty sure that Jed had been badly hurt at some time in his life.

He'd never talked about the trouble he'd been in when he'd left Arizona, and she'd figured it was too painful for him to share with anyone. Now he was determined to go back and try to impress them with his champion buckle and a make-believe wife. Kristi couldn't imagine why the wife bit was so important.

If there was one thing Kristi knew about, it was the futility of trying to impress anyone who didn't want to be impressed. She was afraid that if Jed went back, he'd be hurt again. Maybe, if she went along with him, she might be able to prevent that from happening somehow. And she'd get to find out what it was that Jed had taken such pains to keep to himself for so long.

In any case, she had nothing better to do right now. She needed time to decide what she wanted to do next with her life, and this would give her something to do while she gave the problem some deep thought.

More than anything, though, the prospect of spending some quality time with Jed, in his hometown and with his family, was just too appealing to resist. Maybe he didn't see her as anything other than a way to settle an old score. At least she was aware of that and as long as she remembered why she was there, she wouldn't get hurt.

"Are you feeling all right?"

Lori's voice startled her, and she looked up, unsettled to find everyone's gaze on her. "Sorry," she muttered, "I was thinking about something."

"Must have been pretty heavy," Cord said, his black gaze intent on her face.

Kristi shrugged. "Guess I'm getting tired. I think I'm going to make tracks for home."

Lori and April apparently agreed, since they both stood up with her. Kristi did her best to focus on the group as the goodbyes were exchanged. Lori and Cord were off to the northwest mountains, while Denver and April were headed for eastern Oregon and the new rodeo school. Plans were made for everyone to join up at April and Denver's wedding the week after Christmas, then after a flurry of hugs, kisses and promises, they drifted off toward the exit, leaving Jed and Kristi alone at the table.

"How did you get here?" Jed asked, as Kristi picked up her purse with a not-too-steady hand.

"I came by cab." She looked at her watch. "I can call for one from the foyer."

"I can give you a ride if you don't mind sitting in the truck in that dress."

She felt a shiver inside as his gaze swept over her with the same unsettling effect he always had on her. "I don't mind."

She left the room, conscious of him walking close by her side as he accepted the congratulations from a group of cowboys standing near the door. She was

aware of their appreciative appraisal as she walked
by them, and it gave her a little surge of triumph to
know they approved of the way she looked.

The desert air chilled her, in spite of the light
jacket she'd thrown over her bare shoulders. She
climbed into the cab of the truck, grateful for the
warmth when Jed started up the engine.

They were almost back at her camper when Jed
said quietly, "I don't want to rush you or anything,
but I plan on leaving day after tomorrow. If you're
coming with me, I'll need to know in the morning."

She barely hesitated when she answered him,
though she had trouble dealing with the heady sense
of recklessness. "I've already decided," she said
firmly. "I'll do it. I guess I'll be your make-believe
wife."

Chapter 3

Kristi slept badly that night, waking up several times with a panicky feeling of having burned her bridges. She thought about calling Jed and telling him she'd changed her mind, but always the notion came back to haunt her—this might be her only opportunity to give her relationship with him a chance to develop.

When the alarm finally went off, she climbed out of bed, unhappily aware that she was not going to look her best for her big day. She'd arranged to meet Jed for breakfast, to go over her new role as his make-believe wife. There were things she needed to know, he'd told her last night, if she was going to convince everyone she was Mrs. Jed Cullen.

Just the sound of that had blown her mind, to the extent that she had entirely lost whatever he had said after that. All she remembered was that she was to meet him for breakfast, and if she didn't hurry, she reminded herself with a hasty glance at her travel alarm clock, she'd be miserably late.

She picked out her usual jeans and checkered shirt to wear, needing the assurance of the customary clothes. In spite of them, she felt a distinct sense of unreality as she walked into the pancake house on the Strip, as if she had already cast aside everything that was familiar and had embarked on a strange and somewhat threatening new path.

Jed was already there when she reached the counter. She spied him sitting in a booth next to the window, his hat tipped back on his head as he sipped a mug of coffee. Without waiting for the hostess, she walked over to the booth and slid in opposite him.

He looked up, and her heart leapt at the glint in his golden eyes. "I thought you might have changed your mind."

She shook her head, unable to come up with one of her usual flip comments. She felt ridiculously shy and uneasy, and it wasn't a familiar sensation. Usually she was never at a loss for words, the smart answer, the quick comeback. But ever since she'd heard Jed refer to her as Mrs. Jed Cullen, she'd been unable to escape the quivering sense of intimacy those words aroused.

No matter that it would be a farce, a charade put on to fool the people of Promise. No matter that Jed's motivations for such a pretense had nothing to do with the way he felt about her. No matter that once it was over she'd probably never see Jed Cullen again. Just the thought of what their little ruse would entail made her heart thump and her pulse skitter about like kittens in a cornfield.

Her silence must have made Jed nervous. He narrowed his eyes, and leaned toward her across the table. "You haven't, have you?"

She blinked. "Haven't what?"

"Changed your mind."

"I wouldn't be here if I'd changed my mind," she said lightly.

When she glanced back at him he had leaned back in his seat, apparently satisfied. "Good. We have a lot to go over before we get to Promise, but most of it I can tell you while we're driving there. There's a couple of things we have to take care of first, though."

"Like what?"

The waitress moved over to their table at that moment, and flipped a page over on her pad. "What can I get for you this morning?" She cast a bored glance at Jed, then widened her eyes. "You're Jed Cullen, aren't you?"

Jed gave her a heartbreaker smile. "I was the last time I looked."

"I saw you win the all-around buckle on Sunday. That was some ride."

Kristi kept quiet as the waitress chattered on about how she'd followed Jed's career.

Jed answered her with good humor, making the woman laugh with his dry comments.

Finally, Kristi decided she'd had enough. Before the waitress could launch into another avalanche of questions, she said loudly, "Honey, don't you think

we'd better order now? My gut is growling I'm so
hungry.''

Jed frowned, while the waitress sniffed loudly,
gave Kristi a cool look and demanded, ''So what will
it be?''

Jed waited until the waitress had disappeared with
their order before saying, ''You'll have to work on
that.''

She stared at him. ''Work on what?''

''The way you talk.''

''What the heck's the matter with the way I talk?''

''It's not ladylike.''

Kristi struggled to keep her resentment under control when she answered him. ''You're trying to tell
me it's not the way rich people talk.''

His frown cleared. ''Exactly. I'm glad you understand that. Now personally, I've got nothing at all
against the way you talk. Hell, I talk that way myself.
But if I'm going back to Promise with a classy
woman for a wife, you'll have to learn how to talk,
act and look like one.''

She lifted her chin. ''Why'd you bother asking me
if I'm not good enough?''

He sighed. ''Look, Kristi, I'm not putting down
the way you talk. I'm just saying that if we want to
fool the people of Promise you just can't go around
acting like a stock handler for the rodeo. Above all,
you can't tell anyone you work for the rodeo.''

''Why not? Is it something I should be ashamed
of?''

He pursed his lips. ''Maybe I shouldn't have asked
you to do this.''

Her desire to go on this adventure with him out-weighed her pride. Drawing a deep breath she said quietly, "All right. I guess I understand what you're saying. It's just that I don't know if I can do all that... You know, act like a high-society lady. I've never been around anyone like that."

"What about your father? He owns the stockyards. He's got plenty of money. He must have women friends like that."

Kristi shook her head. "Dad has never looked at another woman since Mom died. Even if he did, I don't think he'd pick someone with all the airs and graces you talk about. He's as down-to-earth as any of the cowboys that ride on the circuit. That's where I learned everything I know...including the way I talk, I reckon."

"No, you learned all that from being around cow-boys and rodeo folk all your life." Jed's eyes crin-kled as he softened his words with a smile. "No offense, Kristi, but you act more like a man than a woman. Except when you're all fancied up like you were last night. Then you could pass for a high-class woman."

Kristi bit back an angry retort. All this might be easier to understand if she knew why it was so all-fired important for Jed. He wasn't volunteering any information, however, and she sensed this wasn't a good time to ask. "All right, tell me what I need to do, then."

"You're gonna have to get some new clothes, for one thing."

She eyed him suspiciously. "What kind of clothes?"

"Like you had on last night."

"Are you nuts? If I ride into town in the middle of the day dressed like that, all your precious townsfolk are gonna take me for a freaking hooker."

Jed winced. "You'll probably cinch it talking like that."

She let out her breath on a sigh of exasperation. "This isn't gonna work, is it? There's no way I can pull it off."

"Of course it'll work. We'll make it work." He reached out and patted her hand. "You'll get the hang of it, you'll see. You're a knockout when you're dressed up, with all that stuff on your face. All you have to do is watch your language and you'll be fine."

She looked at him, doubts still crowding her mind. "If I can't tell them I work at the rodeo, where do I work?"

"You don't. Rich people don't work."

"Of course they do. That's how they get rich."

He wrinkled his brow. "All right, you're a model."

She burst out laughing. "Now I know you're nuts. They're never going to believe that."

"I'd believe it."

Astonished, she said, "That's a real nice thing to say, Jed."

He brushed her comment off with an impatient jerk of his hand. "Now all we need is the clothes. I'll give you some money and you can go shopping this afternoon. Then get packed up and we can be ready to leave by tomorrow morning.''

She blinked. Everything was happening too fast. The feeling of panic was back. ''I don't think I can learn to be ladylike in one afternoon—''

He reached out and this time captured her fingers on the table. She promptly forgot what she was going to say. She could only stare in bemused silence at his strong brown hand clamped over hers.

''Kristi,'' he said urgently, ''I don't have time to wait any longer. I only have a month before I'll be back on the road again, and I need that time to do what I have to do in Promise. Just do the best you can, okay? I know you can do it.''

Right at that moment she'd walk barefoot over hot coals for him. ''Well, all right. But I'm not going to be a model.'' She frowned, trying to think of something she could be that wouldn't be too difficult. ''You know what?'' she said at last. ''I think I'd like to be a buyer for a fancy dress shop. I don't know a whole lot about fashions, but then I reckon people in a small town won't know much, either.''

His relief brought a broad smile to his face as he nodded. ''That's my girl. You're gonna be great, I can tell.''

She wished fervently that she shared his confidence. ''I'm buying my own clothes, though. I don't want you paying for them.''

''Wait a minute, this is my deal and I pay the expenses.''

''You can pay for everything else if you want, but I buy my own clothes.'' If something went wrong, she didn't want to be in his debt. Besides, if she was paying for the clothes, she thought grimly, she'd get to choose them. She had a horrible feeling that if she allowed Jed to pay for them, he'd hover over her all afternoon telling her what to buy.

In any case, she could use a new wardrobe. Thank the stars for credit cards.

"Okay, Cactus. If you insist."

"Cactus?"

"Yeah. On account of you're so all-fired prickly."

She wasn't quite sure she appreciated that, but just then the waitress arrived with plates of food balanced on her arm.

Kristi said nothing while she waited for the waitress to stop fluttering around Jed. Something else had occurred to her, and she wasn't sure how to broach the subject. She waited until they had almost finished their meal before saying hesitantly, "What about the ring?"

Jed looked puzzled. "What ring?"

"Most married women wear a wedding ring."

"Oh, damn, I'd forgotten about that. I guess I'll have to buy one. I'll get the check and we'll go right now."

"We could buy a fake gold ring," she suggested a few minutes later, as they walked out of the restaurant together. "These days it's tough to tell the difference."

"Until your finger turns blue and falls off." He took hold of her arm and steered her across the road toward the entrance of a fancy hotel. "There should be a jewelry store in here."

She reached the sidewalk and halted. "You can't buy a ring in there. It will cost you a fortune. We can find a small jewelry store on the edge of town—"

"We're going in here."

Once more he grasped her arm, and pulled her onto a moving walkway that transported people past pristine pools and fountains into the magnificent entrance of the hotel. Kristi would have lingered to explore the fascinating scene surrounding them, but Jed spotted a jewelry store tucked away at the far end of the plaza and urged her over there.

"That one," he announced, pointing to a tray of wedding rings beneath the glass counter.

The heavily perfumed woman reached for the tray and delicately placed it on the counter. "Perhaps Madam would care to try it on?" she murmured.

Madam was only too happy to slip the diamond-studded ring on her finger. It just happened to be a perfect fit, and she stared at it, fascinated by the look of it on her hand. It sat there glittering at her, its brilliance mocking her for the absurdity of the situation. "It's lovely," she said breathlessly. "But much too expensive."

She started to draw it off, but Jed spread his fingers above her hand. "We'll take that one," he said firmly.

The woman stretched out her hand for it. "I'll put it in a box for you." She glanced at Jed. "Would the gentleman care to have the matching ring?"

"Oh…I…no, I don't wear rings," Jed said hastily.

The woman gave him a disapproving look. "Very well, sir," she said stiffly. "I'll be right back."

Kristi watched her disappear behind a black curtain, then whispered, "That's too much to pay for a pretend ring. What are you going to do with it afterwards?"

"Consider it a gift. For helping me out."

His unexpected generosity stunned her and she was silent as they waited for the woman to return with a small box. She slipped the box into a gold paper bag and handed it to Jed, then she took the credit card he offered her and finished the transaction.

"Thank you, sir," the assistant said, as she handed Jed the sales slip. "Here is your certificate. Congratulations, and I hope you'll both be very happy."

"Yeah, sure," Jed muttered, and headed for the door.

Kristi gave the woman a bright smile, and received a pitying look from her in return. Obviously the elegant assistant didn't think much of Jed's attitude toward his prospective bride.

Kristi hurried out of the shop and caught up with Jed, who seemed to have forgotten he'd left her behind. "You'll have to work on that," she said breathlessly, as she kept pace with him along the busy arcade.

He glanced down at her. "On what?"

She wasn't sure how to put it. "Well, you'll have to act more romantic if you want people to think we're newlyweds."

His eyebrow rose a fraction of an inch, but otherwise he hung on to his stoic expression. "I'll manage when the time comes," he said shortly. He thrust the gold bag at her. "Here, you might as well get used to wearing this."

She took it, feeling a faint sense of disappointment that he hadn't made more of a ceremony of it. She immediately scolded herself for being such a fool. This was a business arrangement. A deal made between friends. If she wanted to come out of this without getting hurt she'd better remember that.

The rest of the day flew by as she shopped for decent clothes to take with her to meet Jed's folks. She was careful to buy stuff she knew she'd use once the charade was over...mostly well-cut pants and silk shirts, a suede jacket, a couple of dresses and shoes, and a long skirt with a provocative slit up the side.

Jed had made arrangements and paid the fee to park her camper next to his in a small trailer park. She was to meet him there in the morning, and then they would drive to Arizona in a rented car. She went to bed that night certain that excitement and nervousness would keep her awake, but when she awoke in the morning to the strident buzz of her alarm she felt refreshed and ready for her new adventure.

An hour later she steered the big camper into the trailer park and looked for space number sixteen, which Jed had told her would be her spot until they returned from Promise.

Jed's camper was already parked in the spot next to hers, but there was no sign of his rangy figure when she climbed down from the front seat, and her thump on the door went unanswered. She settled down to wait for him, and a few minutes later she was intrigued to see a bright red sports car roar into the park with Jed at the wheel.

He pulled up alongside her camper and gave her a jaunty wave. She waited for him to climb out, then gave the car an approving nod. "Nice."

He grinned. "This should make the citizens of Promise sit up and take notice, right?"

She raised her eyebrows. "You must really want to impress them."

His grin faded. "You bet I do. Besides, this was a little gift I promised myself if I won the championship. I've been saving my pennies for a long time."

"Don't you think it's time you told me why you're so determined to make such a grand entrance?"

"I will. On the way." He looked her over, as if seeing her for the first time. "You look good."

She felt warmed by the compliment. "Thanks. I should, considering what this little outfit cost."

"Are you ready to roll?" He glanced at her camper. "Where are your bags?"

"Just inside the door. I'll get them."

"No, you get in the car. I'll get them."

Normally she would have protested, asserting her independence, but just in time she remembered her new role as his pampered wife and meekly handed him the keys, then climbed into the car to wait for him. He returned a few minutes later and stuffed her luggage into the undersized trunk before climbing in next to her.

There wasn't a lot of room between the seats, and

his arm bumped hers as he reached forward to put the key into the ignition. The contact made her jump, and she automatically shifted her body away from him.

He sent her a sideways glance. "It's gonna be a little tough to be romantic if you leap away from me whenever I get close to you."

She felt her cheeks burn. "I was just giving you more room."

"Uh-huh. How come you're not wearing the ring?"

She shrugged. "I thought I'd wait until we get to Promise."

"Well, I reckon if we're gonna act like husband and wife, we should start practicing now."

She looked at him suspiciously. This was a complete turnaround from the day before. "Practicing?"

"Yeah, you know…talk and act like married people."

She thought about that. "I'm not sure I know how married people talk."

"Well, like Cord and Lori…act like them."

Her pulse twitched. She remembered the loving glances between the two newlyweds—the way they touched each other, the quick kisses when they thought no one was looking. "But they've only just got married," she said weakly.

"So have we. I can't go back to my folks and tell them I got married months ago and didn't let them know about it. I figure on telling them we got married yesterday, after the finals."

"Oh." She hadn't bargained on acting like a honeymoon couple. This charade promised to be even more interesting than she'd imagined.

She thought about it while Jed took the dusty road out of town and headed toward Arizona. As they drove, she tried to imagine herself acting naturally when Jed got romantic. The more she thought about it, the more jittery she felt.

After they'd been driving for an hour or so, Jed broke a long silence to ask if she was thirsty. "There's a pretty good truck stop just around the bend," he told her. "We can get lunch and a glass of beer if you want."

"Sounds good," she told him, relieved at the prospect of relaxing with other people around. It seemed ironic that after all the time she'd spent dreaming of being alone with Jed, now that it was actually happening she felt like a kid on her first day in school— uncertain and out of her depth. She just hoped she could keep her head, and not read anything into whatever happened once they were in Promise. She had to hang on to reality, and remember that this was just a pretense...or she could end up really getting hurt.

To her relief, all the time they were at the truck stop, Jed acted the way he normally did when they were together. She'd been half-afraid he'd start practicing right there in front of everyone. He teased her about the way she drank her beer, and told her she'd have to learn to drink wine if she was going to act like a high-class lady.

When they left the restaurant, she tried to smother her little surge of resentment. He meant well, and she knew how anxious he was for her to fool everyone. Yet his teasing rankled.

She was surprised when a short time later, he pulled over to the side of the road and stopped the car. "There's something you should know before we hit town," he said, looking straight ahead with his hands resting on the wheel. "I figured it would be best if I didn't have to concentrate on driving while I'm talking."

Apprehension stirred in her stomach as she looked at his bleak face. She guessed he was about to tell her the reason he was going back to Promise, and she knew it wouldn't be easy for him to talk about it.

She waited, hardly daring to breathe, until he said quietly, "There's no other way to say this except to come right out and say it. I got into some trouble when I was a kid."

He paused, as if expecting her to say something.

Not sure what he wanted from her, she asked warily, "What kind of trouble?"

"When I was in my senior year of high school I was arrested for armed robbery."

His words wiped out anything she might have said at that moment. She didn't know what she'd expected to hear, but it wasn't this. She stared at him, unable to associate this man with something as bad as the crime he'd mentioned. When he didn't speak, she realized he was waiting for her reaction. She took a deep breath, then said unsteadily, "There had to be some mistake. I can't believe you would do something like that."

He looked at her then, and her heart skipped at the expression in his eyes. "Thanks for giving me the benefit of the doubt. Maybe if other people had done the same thing back then, my life might have been a whole different story."

She felt a strong urge to touch his face, to reassure him. "Tell me about it."

He was quiet again for too long, then finally he sighed. "There was a robbery at the gas station outside of town. I didn't do it, but I couldn't prove I didn't, and I was arrested."

She felt cold. "What happened?"

He pushed the brim of his hat up with his thumb and leaned back in his seat, staring straight ahead through the windshield. "It all started when I took a fancy to Sarah Hammond. She was in my senior-year class, and just about every guy there wanted to date her.

"Sarah had everything," he said, his voice softening. "Looks, money and a sweet, funny personality that completely blew the mind of a hick country boy from the wrong side of the tracks."

Kristi took an immediate dislike to Sarah Hammond. "Go on," she said.

"Well, her father was a lawyer, and her mother was some kind of psychologist, I think. Anyway, she was so far beyond my world, I never figured she'd give me a second look. But one day I came around a corner too fast, and there she was, right in front of me."

This time he paused for so long she was irritated. "And?" she prompted.

Jed stirred. "Sorry, I was trying to remember how I got the nerve to ask Sarah for a date. She'd dropped her books and I picked them up, and the next thing I knew, we had a date for the next night."

Kristi did her best to bury the resentment she felt. It was a long time ago, she assured herself. Obviously things hadn't worked out between them. "So you took her out?"

"Yep." He uttered a dry laugh. "I can still remember how scared I was that night. I'd never been up close to someone like Sarah before. I was so worried I'd say the wrong thing and look stupid. Anyway, we ended up on Coldstone Peak. It's a spot in the hills where you're up high enough to see clear across the desert to the lights of Phoenix."

"Sounds real nice," Kristi muttered.

Jed shrugged. "I thought it was. Anyway, I asked Sarah to go steady. I knew she was hooked up with Rory Madison at the time, but I figured if he wasn't man enough to hold on to her, he deserved to lose her. Besides, the kid was a jerk. Sarah didn't belong with someone like him."

"Who was Rory Madison?"

"Well, I guess you could say the Madisons own the town of Promise. Rory's great-great-something grandfather settled the town after the Civil War when he found silver in the hills. Rory got this idea that the Madisons owned everyone in town, just because his family owned the refinery, and built a couple of schools and a clinic."

"What you'd call a prominent citizen," Kristi said.

"Yeah, I reckon. Anyway, Rory found out about Sarah and me. I reckon the whole town knew since we were together just about every night. Things were getting pretty serious between Sarah and me—until one day Rory was waiting for me when I came out of school."

"Oh-oh," Kristi said anxiously. "What happened?"

Jed sighed. "Well, he started throwing his weight around, threatening me and calling me names, saying bad stuff about my family...so I bopped him."

Kristi grinned. "How hard?"

"Not hard enough," Jed muttered. "But it was a pretty good fight, and I reckon I left him with a few bruises. I figured his father might call my father and complain, but I never expected the sheriff to show up."

"The sheriff? You're kidding."

Jed shook his head. "I wish I was. It was a few days after the fight. I'd begun to think that Rory had forgotten about it. I thought it was strange, since the last thing he yelled at me when he was spitting blood was that he was going to get even."

Thoroughly intrigued now, Kristi leaned forward. "So what happened?"

"The sheriff told me he was arresting me for the armed robbery of the gas station outside of town."

"Oh my, that must have been a shock."

"It was. I thought it was a joke and Rory had put him up to it, at first. Until he clapped handcuffs on me and put me in the car. That's when I realized he was dead serious. When I got to the sheriff's office, he told me that Boomer Carson, the guy who worked at the gas station, had been hit on the head and knocked out. Whoever did it took the money out of the cash register. There wasn't a whole lot of cash, as I recall, but Boomer got a concussion and was in hospital. When he'd woken up he'd told the sheriff that he had his back to the door when the robber went in, but he saw the thief's reflection in the window opposite. It was Halloween night, and the robber was wearing one of those rubber face masks. He was also carrying a gun."

"What made him think the robber was you?"

"I guess his height and weight were pretty close to mine. Anyway, before Boomer could turn around and get a good look, he was hit."

"The sheriff arrested you because you were the same weight and height as the robber?"

"No," Jed said quietly. "He arrested me because he found a gun and a face mask buried in my backyard."

She stared at him, his words sounding so unbelievable she thought at first he must be joking. She only had to look at his face, however, to know he wasn't teasing this time. It was hard to imagine someone having hated this man enough to frame him for such a serious crime. Yet instinct told her that Jed was incapable of using the kind of violence he'd described.

Now she had grave doubts about going back to Jed's hometown. With enemies like that in his past, she couldn't help wondering what kind of trouble was waiting for them in Promise, Arizona.

Chapter 4

"You mean someone actually buried a gun and a mask in your backyard to incriminate you?" Kristi shook her head in disbelief. "You think Rory did it?"

"I know he did it," Jed muttered. "Trouble was, back then I could never prove it. I suggested to the sheriff that he ask Rory about it. But Rory was a Madison, son of the founding fathers of Promise, Arizona, and I was just the son of a refinery worker. Rory's father paid my father's wages."

"That shouldn't have made any difference."

"You don't know the people of Promise. According to them, the Madisons can do no wrong. It was my word against Rory's, and my word didn't count for very much. My accusing him just made everything look worse for me. After all, the sheriff had found the evidence buried in my backyard and I already had a bad name as a troublemaker.''

Kristi looked at him in surprise. ''Troublemaker? You?''

Jed nodded. ''I used to talk with my fists in those days. I'd been in trouble a couple of times in school for fighting. Mostly over dumb stuff.''

''I've never seen you raise your hand against anyone.''

''That's why I don't,'' Jed said dryly. ''It's one of the things I promised myself I'd never do again. Anyway, I didn't have an alibi for that night. All my folks knew was that I'd spent the evening in my room. But they always went to bed around ten or so, and the robbery took place at eleven-thirty, right before the station closed. I could have easily left the house after everyone was asleep. In fact, my father said he thought he heard the front door close late that night. That just about clinched it.''

Kristi frowned. ''Your father thought you'd robbed the gas station?''

Jed's mouth hardened. ''Everyone believed it, except for Luke Tucker, my best buddy. Even Sarah believed I was guilty.''

''That must have been very painful,'' Kristi said quietly.

''Yeah, it was. As for my pa, I didn't know how he could think I was capable of robbing a gas station.'' He shook his head. ''I still don't understand it.''

''What about your mother? Surely she didn't believe you were guilty?''

Jed shrugged. "I reckon she didn't know what to believe. She knew I'd been in trouble at school. They'd called her up there a couple of times to discuss my behavior. I guess when the sheriff hauled me off in the car she just gave up on me."

"I'm sorry." Such inadequate words, yet she couldn't find anything else to say that would let him know how badly she felt for him. "So what happened after the sheriff arrested you?"

"Well, like I said, there was the evidence buried in my backyard, there was the fact I was a troublemaker, there was the fact that Rory had an alibi and I didn't—"

She interrupted him. "Rory had an alibi?"

"Yeah. A couple of his buddies swore he was with them the whole evening. Rory went around telling everyone that I wanted Sarah and I'd stolen the money so's I could compete with him and buy her stuff to impress her. Everyone knew we'd had a fight over Sarah, and they said I was trying to put the blame on Rory to get rid of him."

Kristi groaned. "Oh, Lord, what a mess."

"You can say that again," Jed said heavily. "I figured I'd be put away for something I didn't do. I was pretty damn scared, I can tell you. I went before the judge, and I shook so bad I could hardly speak. But there were no prints on the gun, and Boomer couldn't identify me for sure. Then there was the fact that I hadn't spent any money since the robbery. The judge ruled it insufficient evidence. I was lucky."

Kristi's heart ached when she saw the pain in his

face. "I'm so sorry," she whispered. "That must have been a terrible experience."

He nodded. "Yeah, it was. I found out afterwards that old man Madison, Rory's father, put in a good word for me. I figured he felt sorry for my family, and didn't want to see them disgraced by having a son in jail. Anyway, he was the only one in town, except for Luke, who had a kind word for me. Like I said, my pa wouldn't believe that I hadn't done it. He ranted on about me being a loser and ruining my life, that no one would ever trust me again. He said he always knew that my temper would get me in trouble one day. He told me I'd lost the one thing that could have made me as good as the Madisons, and that was respect."

Kristi swallowed. "Oh, Jed, that's awful."

Jed's voice was hard and flat when he spoke again. "My mother said that I'd made things bad for Wayne, my kid brother. I guess she was afraid everyone would look down on him, too. No one would believe that Rory had framed me. After all, Rory was a Madison and Madisons didn't do things like that."

"So that's why you left town," Kristi said unsteadily.

"When my family figured I was guilty, and my friends looked at me as if I was no better than dirt, yeah…that's when I left town. I figured there was nothing left to keep me there. I was an outcast. I didn't belong there anymore."

"So you're going back now to try to convince them they were wrong."

"Yeah, I'm going back. This time they'll listen."

Kristi wished she could share his optimism. "Jed, I don't want to burst your bubble, but do you really believe that a championship buckle and a make-believe wife are going to make those people take your word over Rory's?"

His sideways glance held a hint of belligerence. "Maybe not on their own, but I have something else up my sleeve that could sure rock Rory's little boat."

Her pulse quickened. "Like what?"

"Like the key to the gas station."

She frowned. "I don't understand."

Jed leaned back in his seat with a smug expression. "Earlier this year, Luke Tucker came to see me. I hadn't seen nor heard from him since I'd left town. I guess he'd left Promise soon after I did, and never knew I was in rodeo until he happened to see a poster advertising the competition in his hometown in California. We had a couple of drinks together, and he told me that a week or two after I left, he was in a bar and he saw Rory arguing with a buddy of his, Dave Manetti. Dave was one of the jerks who'd lied to give Rory an alibi. He'd been drinking pretty heavily, and Luke figured he just might feel like talking. So he bought Dave a couple more drinks and asked some pretty leading questions. Dave wouldn't say anything at first, until Luke warned him that Rory would sell him down the road just like he did me. That's when Dave showed him the key."

"The key to the gas station?"

"Uh-huh. Luke saw the tag on it. Dave wagged that little sucker in front of Luke's face and told him it was the key to his future. As long as he had that, he told Luke, he had Rory right where he wanted him.''

''Where'd he get the key from?''

Jed shrugged. ''Luke asked him that. Dave wouldn't tell him, but he did say that if Rory knew he had it, he'd lose more than a night's sleep. Luke figured it had something to do with the robbery, so after Dave had a few too many and wasn't paying attention, Luke took the key from him. It was Luke's last night in town, he was leaving for California the next morning, so he took the key to my pa, and told him to take it to the sheriff.''

Kristi stared at him in dismay. ''Your dad didn't believe him?''

Jed shrugged. ''I guess not. When Luke went back a few years later he went to see pa. Pa wouldn't even talk to him. Luke knew that without the key he wouldn't have a chance of convincing the sheriff, so when he saw that poster he figured he'd tell me about it.''

''Do you think your dad still has the key?''

''I don't know,'' Jed said grimly. ''But I sure aim to find out.''

''But it will still be your word against theirs.''

''Maybe. But with that key in my hand I have a better chance of convincing Dave Manetti that I know enough to get him into real trouble unless he tells me what really happened. The championship and a wife will give me that respect the townsfolk are all so damn concerned about, and I reckon they'll be more likely to listen to me now.

''I hope you're right.'' In that moment her heart

ached for him. She'd glimpsed in Jed Cullen something she thought she'd never see...a sense of vulnerability that was in stark contrast to his tough, indomitable image.

The notion so moved her she acted on impulse, answering to her natural instinct to comfort. She leaned over, reached for his jaw, turned his face toward her and kissed him full on the mouth.

She felt his momentary resistance, then the earth exploded when he pulled her closer and turned the light caress into something far more potent and passionate. This was what she'd imagined so many times in the past. This was what she'd waited for, longed for, dreamed of...and it was every bit as devastating as she'd expected.

Kissing Jed Cullen was like taking a ride to the moon—exhilarating, a little frightening and more erotic than anything she could have imagined. His mouth was warm and hard, yet soft at the same time, and she wondered how that could be. This was different from anything she'd ever felt before, and she gave herself up to the sheer joy of the moment. To hell with worrying about getting hurt. This was the man she wanted...had wanted ever since she'd first set eyes on him, and somehow, in the next few days she'd make him see that they were perfect for each other.

The kiss seemed to last forever, and at the same time ended much too soon. Kristi looked up into Jed's face, and saw fire in his eyes for a brief moment before he let her go with a low laugh.

"I reckon that wasn't bad for our first practice

session,'' he said, his voice deliberately casual. ''I guess we'd better make a move if we want to make Promise before dark.''

Kristi nodded, determined not to let him know that she felt as if she'd walked into an icy waterfall in the middle of winter. Obviously the kiss hadn't meant a fig to him. When was she going to learn that men like Jed Cullen didn't go for women like Kristi Ramsett? What gave her the dumb idea that she was going to change his mind about that? Especially now that he was going back to Promise, and Sarah.

She sank back in her seat, doing her best not to scowl. Sarah Hammond. Things had been serious between them, he'd said. She could see Sarah now: gorgeous green eyes, straight, silky blond hair—not the kind that came out of a bottle, either—and a figure to die for. That would be Sarah Hammond. Kristi hated her already. Was Jed still hung up on her? Was Sarah the real reason he was going back to Promise? Was this whole wife thing just to make Sarah Hammond jealous?

Kristi waited until she was sure she could speak casually about it before asking, ''So, what happened to Sarah after you got arrested?''

Jed shrugged. ''She got engaged to Rory soon after that. That's when I figured out that it paid to have money and power. Sarah was more ready to believe Rory than me because he was a Madison and I was a nobody. I must have been some kind of fool to think she'd choose me over him.''

''No, you weren't a fool. Just young and far too trusting.''

"Yeah, well, it'll be a cold night in hell before I let another woman make a fool of me like that."

She could hardly blame him. But now she knew about Sarah, it looked as if she had more to contend with than she'd first thought. Jed Cullen had a ghost in his past—and a formidable one. She could understand now why he was so determined not to get too close to a woman.

That didn't mean she was giving up, she told herself, in an effort to bolster her sagging spirits. A lot could happen in Promise, Arizona, and just maybe she might be able to help him forget about Sarah and restore his faith in women. Especially if she could help him clear his name.

Right then the determination was born. He hadn't asked her to be his savior, and she was sure that the thought had never occurred to him. But if she could do this thing for him, and help him find the respect and admiration he so badly craved from the people of Promise, then maybe he'd see in her the one woman who could make him happy. Maybe.

Jed was relieved when Kristi lapsed into silence. He didn't want to talk about Sarah. Her betrayal still festered inside him, and probably always would. He wasn't sure how he'd react if he saw her in Promise, and he probably would, he ruefully acknowledged. Right now, however, he had something else to worry about.

He'd been taken aback when Kristi had kissed him, but not nearly as unsettled as he was by his own reaction. For a moment he'd forgotten the fact that she was there because he'd more or less hired her to act as his wife. The uppermost thought in his mind was that Kristi not only felt good in his arms, she smelled great and tasted even better.

In fact, he wasn't too surprised to discover that kissing Kristi was an incredibly satisfying experience. At the same time it generated all kinds of other desires and needs, most of which hadn't been taken care of in quite a while. The thought that Kristi might possibly be able to accommodate him on that level as well set off warning bells in his head. That kind of thinking was dangerous. Even more so, given the fact that they would be sharing a room at the only motel in town.

He'd thought about booking a room in Scottsdale, and commuting to Promise, but he knew if he did that he'd take the edge off his triumphant return. He wanted to be there, in their faces, establishing a presence and making a bold statement about who he was and where he belonged. Which meant sharing a room with Kristi at the Promise Inn.

When he'd first considered the idea of hiring her, he hadn't foreseen that part of the plan as that much of an inconvenience. They'd rent a room with two beds. Simple. He didn't think Kristi was that much of a prude that she couldn't handle a roommate.

His thinking on that had taken a new slant, however, in the light of what had happened just now when they'd kissed. He'd given himself more credit than that, believing himself immune to the fact that she was a woman. Kristi was Kristi, even if she did look like a knockout when she was dressed up. Underneath all that finery, she was still the same woman who could manhandle a frisky heifer back into its pen single-handed while cussing out the miserable wrangler who'd let it loose. At least, that's what he'd figured until now.

So far he hadn't mentioned the subject of where they'd be staying. In another hour they'd be pulling into Promise. It would probably be better for him if he told her now, and give her time to adjust to the idea. Trouble was, he didn't know how to bring up the subject without making it sound like a big deal.

While he was still struggling with the problem, Kristi unexpectedly solved it for him. She pointed out a sign they passed, saying, "Only fifty miles to Promise. Are you getting nervous?"

He was, but not for the reasons she meant. Since he couldn't admit to that, however, he said casually enough, "I guess it will be good to see the folks again. I reckon I won't recognize Wayne. He was only eleven when I left."

"He must be really looking forward to seeing you, too. Especially now that he'll be welcoming a champion back to town."

He cleared his throat. "He doesn't know I'm coming."

She sounded shocked when she spoke. "You didn't tell anyone you were coming back for a visit?"

"Nope. I haven't been in touch with my folks for years."

"Oh, great. How do you think your parents are going to feel when their long-lost son suddenly appears on the doorstep after years of absence with a brand-new wife they've never met and didn't know existed until that moment?''

''Probably better than I felt when they stood by while I was run out of town by false accusations.''

She let out a long sigh. ''You don't have any idea what kind of reception you'll have, do you?''

''Nope.'' He paused. ''Which is why I booked us a room at the inn.'' He waited an uneven heartbeat or two for her reply.

''*A* room?'' she said finally, in a tone a shade higher than normal.

He nodded. ''There's only one motel in town, the Promise Inn. Since it's a real small town, and everyone knows everyone else, if we had separate rooms it wouldn't be long before the whole town knew it. They'd either figure the truth, that we're not really married, or they'd figure the marriage was over before it got a chance to get started, which is more'n likely what they'd expect from a thieving troublemaker like me.''

''Okay,'' she said carefully. ''I get your point. I guess I just hadn't given it much thought until now.'' She paused, then added so quietly he barely heard her, ''Are you sure you want to go through with this wife thing? I mean, I know you figured it would help make you look more respectable and everything, but now that you've had time to think about it, I'd understand if you wanted to change your mind.''

His answer was to pull the car off the road and bring it to a halt on the shoulder. When he looked at her she looked so worried he had to fight the urge to

take her in his arms and kiss away her frown.
"Look," he said firmly, "ever since Denver suggested I take a wife back with me I've been hooked
on the idea. It's exactly what I need to show everyone that I'm just as good as anyone else in town. I
reckon it can't hurt to let people know that someone
like you—or the person you're pretending to be—
believes in me enough to marry me."

She gave him a weak smile. "Okay."

He studied her expression for a long moment.
"There's still time for *you* to change your mind,
though."

"No, I want to do this." She managed a lopsided
grin. "I think it will be fun."

The expression in her eyes suggested she believed
it would be anything but fun. After a moment he
thought he knew what she was worried about.
"Look," he said gruffly. "About the room. We'll
get two beds. I won't...you know...I'm not expecting you to—"

"Oh, I know," she interrupted hastily. "I didn't
think you would. I mean...I wasn't thinking anything
like that...."

"Well, just so's you know." He cleared his throat.
"Are we all right on this, then?"

She still looked uncomfortable, but her smile was
genuine when she held out her hand. "We're all
right. We've got a deal."

He took her hand in his, marveling at how someone as strong as Kristi could have such small, delicate bones. "Deal. Let's knock 'em dead, Cactus.
Now, will you put that ring on your finger?"

She opened the shoulder bag on her lap and took out the small box from the jeweler's. He watched her slip the ring on her finger, and turn it to catch the light. Something warm stirred deep inside him, and he hastily started the car again before he got any more dangerous ideas about Kristi Ramsett.

Kristi spent most of the next half hour trying to get used to the idea of spending the next few days with Jed in a motel room. When he'd first mentioned his plan to her, she'd assumed they would only have to keep up the pretense while in the presence of his family. It hadn't occurred to her that the eyes of the entire town would be on them, to the point where they'd have to share a room. She should be thankful they wouldn't be staying at his family's house, she told herself, as the flickering lights that had twinkled in the darkness ahead of them for the past few minutes separated into the lights of a town. That could have been even more embarrassing—to share a room under the watchful eye of his parents.

"We'll book into the inn," Jed said, as they passed the outlying houses of Promise. "Then we'll go pay my folks a visit."

Kristi's stomach seemed to roll over. "All right," she said cautiously. "But don't you think it would be better if you pay that first visit by yourself? It might be easier on everyone."

"No, I want you with me."

She didn't answer him, and after a minute or two he added quietly, "Are you all right with that?"

"About as all right as I'm going to be," she said

honestly. "I'd be lying if I said I'm not nervous about meeting your folks. What if they ask me questions I can't answer?"

He uttered a short, humorless laugh. "You know far more about me now than they do. If they start talking about the past, just tell them I never talked much about it. Which is no more than the truth."

"I don't know much about your personal likes and dislikes, and you don't know mine. Maybe we'd better go over a few of them before we get there."

He sighed. "You're partial to horses, country music, a good steak and light beer. Probably in that order. You don't like dressing up much, but you'll get up on a dance floor to join a line. You'll laugh at a good joke, but you don't like it much when the boys get smutty. You can handle livestock as well as any wrangler, you can't stand anyone mishandling an animal, and you never, ever cry."

She blinked, surprised he knew that much about her. "Doesn't sound much like a department-store buyer to me," she said unsteadily.

He swore under his breath. "You're right. I almost forgot. Okay, tell me what you think a department-store buyer would like."

She closed her eyes to think better. "Good clothes, expensive makeup and perfume, late-model cars, lobster and martinis."

To her delight, he grinned. "Can you handle that?"

"If you can."

"I reckon we're soon gonna find out."

She looked out the window as he pulled into a

parking lot, and saw an attractive four-story building with black Tudor-style beams decorating the front and an impressive entrance with revolving glass doors. She'd imagined something far smaller and rustic, and was pleasantly surprised.

"This looks very nice," she commented, trying not to reveal the sudden attack of nerves that made her mouth dry and her palms damp. The full implications of her situation were just beginning to make themselves felt. She would have to live with Jed as his wife for the next few days...sharing a room, if not a bed. Now that she was actually facing the prospect, she wasn't at all sure she could handle it.

"This is the only hotel in town," Jed told her as he led her up the steps to the foyer. "The Madisons had it built back in the sixties, when they put all their money into producing an annual rodeo. The only time it's full is when the rodeo is on, but a lot of businessmen use it on their way in and out of Phoenix. And the locals eat out at the restaurant. I reckon it's paid for itself over the years."

The receptionist behind the counter made no attempt to hide her curiosity. "You folks on vacation?" she asked, as she took Jed's credit card.

"Visiting family," Jed said shortly.

The young girl's eyes widened. "Really? Who's your family? I might know them."

"The Cullens. They live out by Partridge Creek. At least I guess they still do."

The receptionist studied Jed's face. "I know the Cullens. At least, I know Wayne. He comes in here now and again for dinner."

Jed nodded. "He's my brother."

The girl stared at Jed, then at the credit card in her hand. "You're Jed Cullen? The rodeo champion?"

"That's me."

Kristi smiled at the satisfaction in his voice, but the girl looked nervously over her shoulder as if she were uneasy about something. "I didn't know you were coming back to town," she said, as she finished processing the credit card. "Wayne didn't mention anything about it."

"I plan on surprising him." Jed took the credit slip from her and put it into his pocket.

"I reckon everyone will be surprised." The girl gave Kristi a thorough appraisal before adding, "No one figured they'd ever see you back in this town again."

Something about the way she said it made Kristi's skin prickle with apprehension. She glanced at Jed's set face and knew he'd sensed it, too.

"Do I know you?" he asked abruptly.

The girl nodded. "You know my family. I'm Betty May Pittman."

Jed shook his head. "I should have known. You're all grown up. I didn't recognize you."

The girl shrugged. "I was just a little kid when you left town, but I guess the folks still remember you. Especially now that you made champion. Kind of brings the memories back, I reckon. My dad says that robbery was the first time we ever had a big crime in Promise."

Jed had his back toward Kristi, but she saw his shoulders stiffen. "Got the key?" he asked gruffly.

The receptionist took a key out of a drawer and handed it to him. "Number 314. Third floor, turn right from the elevator."

He took the key and handed it to Kristi. "Here, you go on up and I'll get the bags."

Remembering her role, she took the key and gave him a warm smile. "Don't be too long, honey," she murmured, in what she hoped was a wifely voice.

Jed's eyebrow twitched, then he leaned in and dropped a swift kiss on her mouth. "I'll be just as quick as I can, sweetheart."

Kristi was glad the receptionist didn't speak to her as she made her way to the elevator. She didn't know if she was more shaken by Jed's kiss, or the callous way the young girl had mentioned the robbery.

All the way up in the elevator she worried about the effect the receptionist's words might have had on Jed. All she could hope was that the rest of the townsfolk weren't as insensitive.

She found the door to their room and opened it. The first thing she noticed was the two queen-sized beds, and breathed a sigh of relief. At least she'd have some respite, since there'd be no need for Jed to act like the eager husband when they were alone in the room. Even so, the sight of those beds so close together made her skin sizzle with anticipation.

She marched to the mirror and took a good look at herself. She'd used a light smattering of makeup, since she wasn't used to wearing it in the daytime. She'd pulled her hair back and tied it at her nape with a black ribbon, going for a sophisticated look. What the style actually did was make her look se-

vere, as well as older. With an irritated grunt, she
pulled the ribbon off and shook her hair free. She'd
have to find a better style, she thought, lifting the
strands with one hand.

She was still experimenting when she heard a
hefty bang, as if someone had kicked the door.
''Open up,'' Jed's voice demanded.

She flew to the door and dragged it open, her
heartbeat quickening when Jed stepped into the room
and dropped the bags onto the floor. She shut the
door behind him, feeling suddenly as if she'd been
abandoned on a distant planet without any way of
getting back.

''I'll unpack this,'' she said breathlessly, and took
hold of her suitcase to drag it over to one of the beds.

''No time.'' Jed looked at his watch. ''I thought
we'd go down and grab something to eat, then go
over to the folks' house. If I know anything about
this town, everyone in it will know I'm back by tomorrow. If they don't already. My folks will want to
know why I didn't go over there first.''

''I'll just tie my hair up again,'' she murmured,
''and wash my hands.''

''No, leave your hair like that. I like it.''

She stared at him, delight fizzing up inside her at
the unexpected compliment. For a moment his gaze
lingered on hers, and she felt the warmth of it sending a glow throughout her body, then he turned way,
saying gruffly, ''You take the bathroom first. I'm going to call them and let them know we're coming.''

Sensing that he wanted to be alone to make what
had to be an emotional call, she took advantage of

the time to refresh her makeup. When she finally emerged, Jed was sitting on the furthermost bed, a scowl marring his face.

Her pulse gave an uneasy jump, and she said carefully, "So, how did it go?"

He shrugged. "I talked to my mom. She didn't sound all that happy to hear from me."

She wanted so much to go over to him and put her arms around him. Instead, she sat on the edge of the other bed, not trusting herself to be that close to him yet. "It really isn't surprising, Jed. Your folks haven't heard from you in years, and now here you are, back in town and you didn't even let them know you were coming. What's more, you booked into the hotel with a woman calling herself your wife. It's no wonder they're a little upset with you."

"I wanted to surprise them. Is that so bad?"

She shrugged. "I only know how I would feel if someone I loved disappeared for years, then turned up again without any explanation."

"I didn't exactly disappear. They knew I was going to join the rodeo. I told them when I left."

"Did you also tell them you weren't going to contact them again for fifteen years?"

He took off his hat and threw it on the bed, then ran a hand through his hair. "Sixteen. And you don't understand. When I left, they were glad to see me go. They made it pretty clear that I was an embarrassment to them. I figured I wouldn't talk to them again until they didn't have to feel ashamed of me anymore."

Her throat constricted. She got up and moved over

to sit next to him on the bed. "I"'m sorry," she said softly. "That must have hurt."

"Yeah," he said bitterly. "It hurt. But now I'm back and I brought them the championship. Not just any championship, but the biggest. The best of the best. I figured they'd be proud of me for that, at least."

She patted his arm. "Give them time," she said quietly. "It must be a shock to them to have you back like this. We'll go eat, and by the time we get over to your folks' house, they'll be over the worst of it and ready to welcome you back."

He uttered an ironic laugh. "Somehow I can't see that happening. But you're right, it's time to eat. We'll both feel better after we've fed our stomachs." He grabbed his hat and jumped to his feet. "Come on, Mrs. Cullen, let's go see if this restaurant still knows how to serve up some decent chow."

Mrs. Cullen, she thought, as she followed him out of the door. The name had a nice ring to it. If only she had the right to use it. She squashed the sudden longing and concentrated on trying to remember everything Jed had told her about himself.

The restaurant was quite elegant, decorated in a quiet Victorian style with elegant oil paintings hung on the dark paneled walls. Kristi chattered throughout the meal. She talked about rodeo in general, people in general, anything to take his mind off the black thoughts she knew preoccupied him, and to keep her own mind off the ordeal ahead. She couldn't fail to notice the curious glances sent their way, and she wished now she'd worn something a little more dressy than slacks and a shirt.

All too soon the meal was over, and it was time to climb back into the car and drive out to Partridge Creek, which according to Jed was right on the edge of town. On the way he pointed out a few landmarks—the community center, the grade school, the medical clinic and the refinery, all of which bore the name of Madison.

Jed hadn't exaggerated the importance of that family in this town, Kristi thought as she caught sight of yet another building with the name of Madison emblazoned across the front. No wonder he'd had trouble convincing the townspeople that the son of their greatest benefactor had committed armed robbery and then framed the son of a refinery worker for the crime.

Her apprehension grew when Jed turned into the driveway of a modest home and parked behind a pickup. She could understand, now, why he was so desperate to make an impression on everyone in town. Even so, she wasn't comfortable about deceiving his family this way. If she'd had the time to really think it through, she might have turned him down. It was too late now, however, and in a way she was glad that she was there to give him some support. Judging by his gloomy expression, he was going to need it.

She stood back a little while he rang the bell, conscious of the heavy thumping of her heart. She prayed that his family would be happy to see him.

She couldn't imagine anyone turning their back on their son, no matter what he'd done. But if they did, if Jed's parents hurt him again the way they'd hurt him in the past, she was very much afraid that this time it would destroy him.

Chapter 5

The door opened, and a pleasant-faced middle-aged woman stood in the doorway. "Jed," she muttered, in a soft voice that Kristi could barely hear. "It's good to see you again."

Kristi felt a lump in her throat as she watched Jed hug his mom. She felt as if she was intruding on a private moment, and looked away, to where the dark sky spread a carpet of stars over the desert mountains.

"This is Kristi, Mom." She felt Jed's hand on her arm and allowed herself to be drawn forward.

Mrs. Cullen's gaze met Kristi's briefly then flicked away again. "Pleased to meet you," she murmured.

Feeling even more uncomfortable, Kristi held out her hand. "I'm happy to know you, Mrs. Cullen. Jed's told me a lot about you."

Jed's mom held Kristi's fingers for a moment and

let them go. She looked up at her son's face, her expression accusing. "I wish I could say the same."

"It all happened so fast, Mom," Jed said heartily. "There just wasn't time."

"Well, don't stand out there in the cold. Come inside."

Jed moved back to let Kristi pass, and she stepped into a small entranceway which led immediately into a large, comfortably furnished room. A man sat in an armchair in front of a blazing fireplace, apparently absorbed in the newspaper that partially concealed his face.

"Dan," Jed's mom called out, a little too brightly, "Look who's here."

The newspaper rustled and a pair of light brown eyes, almost as golden as Jed's, peered over the top of the page behind a pair of gold-rimmed glasses. "Hmmph," Jed's father muttered. "So you're back, then."

Jed's voice sounded strained as he greeted his father. Kristi watched him walk over to the armchair, his hand extended. To her immense relief, Dan Cullen lowered the paper and got to his feet to shake his son's hand. "You look older," he said gruffly. "Been in too much sun, I reckon."

Jed shrugged with a wry grin. "I reckon. You look good, Pa."

Dan Cullen ignored that and sent Kristi a curious glance. "This the new wife, then?"

"Sure is." Jed beckoned her to come over. "Kristi, meet my pa."

Kristi murmured something polite, wondering if it

was appropriate to shake hands with the older man. She could see where Jed got his looks. Dan Cullen was tall and broad-shouldered, with a thatch of thick white hair and blunt features that were still handsome.

He eyed her briefly, then apparently lost interest. "So what are you doing back here?" he demanded, as he sat down again.

Jed nudged Kristi over to a couch, then sat down next to her, laying his hat on the broad arm. "Just came back for a visit. Thought you'd like to meet my wife."

"Too bad you didn't invite us to the wedding."

"It all happened too quickly. Once the rodeo finals were over with, we just decided on the spur of the moment to get hitched."

Dan Cullen nodded. "Yeah, we heard you won the title," he said, in the same voice he might have used to comment on the weather.

Kristi's heart sank when she saw Jed's mouth tighten.

His mom, who had been standing near the door all this time, hurried forward. "Can I get you something to eat? A sandwich, perhaps?"

Jed's voice was bleak when he answered her. "We just ate dinner, Ma."

She was about to answer him when a pounding on the front door interrupted her. "That'll be Wayne," she said hurriedly. "I called him and told him you'd be over." She tugged the door open and a younger version of Jed sauntered into the house.

Wayne Cullen had also inherited his father's looks,

though his hair was lighter than Jed's and his eyes more brown than gold. Although roughly the same height as his brother, Wayne's build was chunkier, softer. He lacked the tough, wiry body, weathered features and aura of restless energy that gave Jed so much of the cowboy image.

"Well, so the bad boy comes home," he murmured, his gaze riveted on Kristi as he approached the couch. "Heard you'd got yourself a knockout of a wife. Reckon they were right." He paused in front of Kristi, reached down for her hand and held it between both of his. "I'm Wayne," he added, giving the length of her body a swift appraisal. "Your new brother-in-law. Welcome to the family."

Kristi didn't care for the way he looked at her, and he was holding on to her hand just a little too long, but he was the first person to make her feel welcome in the house and she gave him a smile. "Thank you, Wayne."

"You can let go of her hand now," Jed said abruptly.

Jed's mother hurried forward again. "Would anyone like coffee?"

Jed raised his eyebrows at Kristi and she shook her head. What she wanted was to leave this house as soon as possible. She could feel the undercurrent of tension and knew Jed felt it, too. She felt angry with both his parents for holding on to their disappointment in him for so long, and for letting him know it.

"Not now, Ma." Jed stood up. "Why don't you sit down here and get to know Kristi."

Kristi did her best to suppress her feeling of panic as Jed's mother gingerly set herself down, while Jed perched one hip on the arm of the couch.

"So, how'd you two meet?" Wayne asked, propping himself up with an elbow on the mantelpiece in front of the fire.

Kristi glanced at Jed's father, who had once more buried himself behind the paper. She felt a surge of resentment.

"We met at a softball game," Jed said, after a short pause.

"Softball?" Jed's mother sounded surprised. "I didn't know you played softball. You were never interested in playing ball games when you were in high school."

"I wasn't playing softball. Kristi was."

"Oh."

Jed's mother snapped her mouth shut and leaned back, giving Kristi a chance to meet Jed's gaze. She hoped he could read her fierce scowl, warning him not to get in too deeply with the lies.

"Well, I'd sure like to see that," Wayne said, in a husky drawl that raised the hair on the back of Kristi's neck.

"That's not very likely," Jed said curtly.

Wayne lifted an eyebrow. "Still got a short fuse, Jed?"

Jed managed a tight smile. "You married yet, Wayne?"

"Married and divorced," Jed's mother answered for him. "I don't know why young people can't stay married nowadays."

"Maybe 'cause they get married in too much of a rush," Dan Cullen muttered from behind his newspaper.

Kristi glanced up at Jed, who winked back at her.

"Where are you working now, Wayne?" he asked. "At the refinery?"

Wayne shook his head. "Heck, no. I'm an electrician. Got my own business."

"Wayne went to technical college," Mrs. Cullen said, with just a trace of smugness in her voice.

"Does Sarah know you're back, Jed?" Wayne asked, a little too casually.

The sudden silence in the room seemed to go on for ever. Then Jed said evenly, "I imagine everyone knows by now."

Wayne grinned. "She'll be shocked to hear you got married in such a hurry. She told me she didn't think you'd ever get married."

Jed's mother gave Kristi a sideways glance that managed to take in her entire body. "You're not pregnant, are you? That's not a very good reason to get married, you know."

"Mom!" Jed protested sharply. "That's none of your business."

Mrs. Cullen lifted her hands from her lap. "If I'm going to be a grandmother I'd like to know about it before the child graduates from high school."

She had a point, Kristi thought. After all, Jed supposedly hadn't bothered to let his family know he was getting married. She reached out and patted his mother's arm. "No, I'm not pregnant. But I promise

I'll let you know the minute I find out that I'm carrying your grandchild.''

The newspaper rustled again, and Dan Cullen said, ''I hope he told you he got arrested for armed robbery a few years back.''

Speechless, Kristi could only stare at him.

''I told her,'' Jed said quietly. ''Kristi and I have no secrets from each other.''

She reached for his hand, striving to give him some comfort.

He squeezed her fingers, and held fast to them as he added, ''Kristi knows I didn't rob that gas station. I reckon Luke Tucker knew it, too. What happened to the key he gave you, Pa? What did you do with it?''

For a moment the paper stilled in Dan Cullen's hands, then he said gruffly, ''Don't know what you're talking about. I don't know nothing about any key.''

''Luke said he gave it to you, Pa.''

There was a note of desperation in Jed's voice that chilled Kristi's heart.

The newspaper descended and Dan Cullen's eyes burned in fierce denial. ''I don't want to talk about it. It was a long time ago and best forgotten.''

''That key could help prove I didn't rob that station.'' Jed jumped to his feet. ''I need that key, Pa.''

''Don't have no key.'' His father disappeared behind the paper again with an air of finality that even Kristi recognized.

''You know Sarah married Rory Madison,'' Wayne said loudly. ''Right after you left town.

They're living up at the big house with his father. His mother died, so Sarah's running the house now. Reckon she'll be real happy to see you back in town.''

"Wayne!" Mrs. Cullen warned sharply. She glanced up at Jed. "Sarah's parents died in a car crash while she was in college. Such a tragedy."

Jed's shock apparently outweighed his frustration with his father. "That must have been real tough on Sarah."

"Yes, it was." Mrs. Cullen turned to Kristi with a tight smile. "What kind of work do you do?"

For a moment Kristi's mind went blank. "I'm a buyer for a department store," she said in a rush, as Jed's gaze bore into her.

"Really?" For the first time, Jed's mother looked straight at her face. "That must be an interesting job."

"It is," Kristi assured her, feeling like a fraud.

"Which department store?"

Once more her mind went blank. She looked up at Jed, furious with him now for putting her in this spot.

"Kristi works for a big chain of stores," Jed said, sounding aggravated. "She travels around a lot."

"Must make it difficult to spend time together," Wayne said softly. "Any time you get lonely, Kristi, you just feel free to call in and visit."

Kristi sent him a cool look. "I never get lonely. I try to attend as many of Jed's competitions as I can. I was there the night he won the all-around championship."

"That was very nice, dear," Jed's mother murmured to no one in particular.

Jed's father simply rustled the pages of his newspaper, while Wayne gave Jed slow grin. "You figuring on blinding us with that buckle, then, Jed?"

Kristi bit back her resentment. She'd deliberately mentioned the championship since no one had paid much attention to the fact that Jed had won it. It was obvious now that his family refused to be impressed by his achievement. Worse, the passing years hadn't seemed to change their belief in his guilt. Even his father had ignored Luke's attempt to convince him of the truth.

All her worst fears had been realized. If the rest of the townsfolk were as determined as his family to ignore Jed's accomplishments and condemn him, then Jed was going to get hurt. Their attitude could open up all the old wounds, from which he might never recover.

Apparently Jed had also realized that he wasn't going to get the approval he was looking for from his family. He stood up abruptly, and reached for his hat. "It's getting late. Reckon Kristi and I will be getting along now."

"You only just got here," Mrs. Cullen complained as she, too rose to her feet.

"We'll be back." Jed strode to the door, barely pausing long enough to say good-night to everyone before ushering Kristi out to the car.

He drove fast on the way back to the inn, his mouth set in a tight, firm line. She tried to think of something to say that wouldn't sound like criticism, and couldn't come up with anything. Jed didn't say a word until he pulled the car into the parking lot of the inn.

"I'm sorry," he said gruffly. "I guess that was pretty tough on you."

"Not nearly as tough as it was on you."

They walked together toward the entrance, their footsteps ringing out in the still night air. "You think I'm wasting my time, don't you?" Jed said.

Caught unawares, she couldn't think of a stock answer. "I think you might have underestimated their reactions a little," she admitted at last.

He started to walk up the steps, his face a cool mask. He didn't speak again until they were inside the room and he'd closed the door. "I should never have brought you into this mess," he said harshly. "It's not fair to you to have to make stuff up and lie like that. It was a stupid idea and I'm sorry I got you mixed up in it. I should have thought about it more, instead of plunging blindly ahead like some fool idiot with half a brain."

She watched him throw his hat on the bed and slump down beside it. "If I remember," she said quietly, "I agreed to come here with you. I knew what I was getting into. I could have turned you down."

"Yeah, well, you didn't know it was gonna be like this."

"Neither did you. I reckon you didn't expect your family would behave that way."

He sighed. "I guess I should have known. I can't

believe my pa won't talk about that key. I was a fool to think anything I did would make any difference.''

She hesitated for a moment, then walked over to the bed and sat down next to him. "There's still time. It might just take a while, that's all. People don't change their way of thinking overnight. You'll convince him, you'll see."

He gave her a bleak look. "I thought that being the rodeo champion might make people more willing to listen to me. You saw my family. They didn't give a damn that I'd won the title. All they could think about was the shame I'd brought on them. If they feel that way, how am I gonna convince anyone else? It's too late to make them think any different."

"No, it's not." In her determination to convince him she grabbed his arm and shook it. "You can't give up before you've even tried. What about Sarah? Maybe she can tell you what really happened that night."

He stared at her, his face once more a cool mask. "Are you saying she knew Rory framed me, and kept quiet about it?"

"She might have been afraid to say anything," Kristi said gently.

"If she covered up for him then, she'll sure as hell do it again, now that she's married to him."

"Did you ever ask her if she knew anything about the robbery?"

"I never spoke to her again after the arrest. I figured it wouldn't do me any good. I guess it was easier for me to think that she believed that I'd robbed the gas station. It would be so much worse if

I thought she'd stood by and let me take the blame for something I didn't do.''

"Rory was a bully. He might have threatened her if she told. Maybe now that she's older, she might be more willing to tell the truth. It's at least worth a shot.''

He stared at her for a long time. Then, to her relief, gave her a slow nod. "All right, Cactus. If you think it's such a good idea, we'll go see her.''

"I think it might be better if you go see her alone. She might be more willing to talk about it if a stranger isn't there.''

The stubborn look she knew well crossed his face. "And how would it look if I visit Sarah Madison without my wife? That would really give the town something to talk about.''

She swallowed. Every time he called her his wife she experienced a major meltdown. It had cost her a lot to suggest he go alone. Much as she wanted to be with him, she was convinced he would get more out of Sarah if she wasn't there. Even so, it was hard to sound convincing when she insisted, "I really do think you should go by yourself.''

He sat looking at her for the longest time with a brooding expression. Finally he let out a long sigh. "Look, I know this is tough on you. Why don't you just go back to Las Vegas and forget about this? I'll make up some excuse…I'll say that you had some kind of big crisis with your job and had to go back. It'll work out fine.''

She wasn't sure if he'd made the suggestion for her own good, or if he felt he'd made a mistake by asking her to come along. "There's nothing for me in Las Vegas," she said carefully.

"So what were you planning on doing before I came along and messed things up for you?"

"You didn't mess anything up. I had planned on spending the next month or two with my father, but I changed my mind. I really didn't have any plans when you invited me to Promise, which is one of the reasons I agreed."

"How come you changed your mind?"

She scowled at him. "I've spent most of my life trying to prove something to my father, and it's all been a complete waste of time. He's never going to be impressed by anything I do."

He gave her a wry smile. "It's not you, Kristi. He just figures that women weren't cut out to do men's work. There's a lot of men out there who think the same way."

She studied him for a minute. "What about you? Is that how you feel?"

He seemed startled by her question. "Heck, no. I know enough about women to know that some of them can handle almost anything. But I'm not your dad."

She shook her head. "I've spent my entire life working toward the day I could take over the stock-yards. Last week he called me to tell me he's put the business on the market. He's selling out."

His expression changed swiftly to sympathy. "Oh, hell. I'm sorry, Kristi. I know how much you wanted to run that business."

She shrugged. "I'll survive. But right now I don't

want to deal with it. I especially don't want to talk about it with my father. I want to help you deal with your problem. You need me. If I leave now that will only give people something else to wonder about. If we're going to make this work we have to make things look as normal as possible. Maybe at least one of us can prove something to the people who matter."

"Well, I think we've got about as much chance of doing that as you have of convincing your father you can run the business. But hell, we might as well give it a shot."

She smiled. "Good for you."

"On one condition."

"And what's that?"

"That we do it together. It's too late to go back on our story now, so we'll have to stick with the married-couple thing, but I'll try not to make it too tough on you, I swear."

The warm feeling was back, and now she felt much better. She held out her hand. "Deal."

"Deal," he answered softly, completely unsettling her when he lifted her hand and pressed his warm lips to the back of it. "Sealed with a kiss."

She wasn't sure what she'd seen flickering in his gaze when he'd answered her. She only knew that his expression was a direct cause of the quivering feeling in her stomach. "I'll take the bathroom first," she said nervously.

He continued to watch her with an odd look in his eyes that threatened to drain all the strength out of her knees. "Okay with me."

She dragged her gaze away and grabbed her overnight bag. "I won't be long."

Once she was safely locked inside the bathroom, she leaned against the wall with sigh of relief. She had to deal with this a whole lot better if she hoped to come out of it with her pride intact. The last thing in the world she wanted Jed to know was that she had a major crush on him. She'd never hear the last of it. She'd be the joke of the circuit, for being fool enough to fall for a guy like Jed Cullen. Trouble was, there was nothing funny about it. The more she was around him, the deeper the hole she was digging for herself.

She was beginning to see a whole new side to Jed, one that she'd bet her boots only a few people had ever seen. The fun-loving, hard-headed cowboy was hiding a lot of controlled emotion under that affable exterior.

She'd once told Lori that Jed never took anything seriously. She knew now how wrong she'd been. The clown was crying inside, and she'd been privileged to see it. The knowledge added a sense of intimacy to their friendship that had never been there before.

Up until now, her relationship with Jed had been more stormy than anything. She'd resented his teasing, even though she knew he hadn't meant any harm by it. She'd thought him insensitive, but now she realized that he used that image to escape from the boy who had been hurt so badly by the people he loved.

To see that vulnerability in such a strong personality was a revelation, and went a long way toward intensifying her feelings for him. Much more of this and she'd be kidding herself that she wasn't in love with him.

The thought made her shiver, and she turned on the shower, determined to keep her resolve not to fall for Jed's undeniable charm. Somehow she had to keep her head if she was going to come out of this unscathed. Something told her that wasn't going to be as simple as she'd imagined.

Outside, in the bedroom, Jed lay back on the bed and covered his eyes with his arm. He'd waited so long for this day. Sixteen long years. He'd played the scenes over and over in his mind…his triumphant return, his family welcoming him with open arms, his father slapping him on the back, townsfolk stopping to greet him on the street and congratulate him, admire his car and envy him his elegant wife.

He'd imagined himself meeting Rory again, and rubbing his nose in the fact that he, Jed Cullen, was a success, in both his personal and his professional life. Now, judging by the reception he'd received so far, it didn't look as if that was going to happen. He didn't even have the key to use against Dave Manetti.

True, he hadn't met too many residents of Promise, other than his family, but right now things didn't seem too promising. On top of everything else, he'd put Kristi in an uncomfortable position, and that upset him. When he'd asked her to pose as his wife, he'd figured on her getting respect and admiration from everyone. But his father had acted as if he felt sorry for her, his mother had been suspicious of her and his brother had treated her like some cheap groupie from the local tavern.

The problem was, he couldn't get her out of it now without making things worse. All he could do was hope like hell she didn't get the same treatment from the rest of the people in Promise. If so, he might have to break a head or two...and that would only reinforce the bad opinion everyone already had of him.

The door of the bathroom opened, shattering his thoughts. He rolled over, and then froze, his breath caught in his throat.

Kristi stood at the side of the other bed, in the act of pulling back the covers. She'd pulled her hair loose from the ponytail and it was fluffed around her face like a shiny blond halo. The pajamas she wore were the color of wood smoke. The silky fabric was pasted against her body like a second skin, outlining every mouthwatering curve.

His own body's reaction was swift and predictable. Aware that the snug jeans he wore would hide nothing from her if she happened to look, he shot off the bed and headed for the bathroom. He managed to shuffle over to his bag with his back to her, then snatched it up and leapt for the bathroom. He could feel the heat in his face when he closed the door and locked it. She must think he was a complete idiot. But one more second out there with her and he could have really messed up.

He just couldn't think straight when she looked like that. It was like being with a different woman. And he did mean woman. The Kristi he was used to seeing had been so much part of the background that he'd barely noticed she was female. The woman out there couldn't hide that fact, even if she draped a potato sack around her.

He didn't know what it was exactly that had changed so much. It was more than the hair, the makeup or even the clothes. It was more…attitude. He stared at himself in the mirror as if the image there could make sense of what he was thinking.

Kristi had changed. He wasn't sure how, or why, but if he'd known she was going to bug him this badly he'd have thought twice about asking her to share a hotel room. It was laughable, really. Here he was, in the perfect place to spend a hot night with a woman who could light his fire, and that woman had to be Kristi Ramsett.

If there was one thing he knew about Kristi, he only had to make one step in the wrong direction and she'd more'n likely haul off and sock him in the jaw. He'd seen her do it once, and he'd never forgotten it. She'd put the poor bastard flat on his back. True, the guy had been drinking. Even so, Jed had made a mental note right there and then never to mess with Kristi in that way.

Kristi wasn't the kind of woman who could spend a night in bed with a man and walk away in the morning. And Jed Cullen never messed with any other kind. In any case, he had enough problems on his mind without worrying about women. Period.

Having settled that, he ran the shower, taking care to keep the water on the cool side. By the time he emerged from the bathroom he was back in control, with his discomfort reasonably alleviated.

To his immense relief, all he could see of Kristi was her tousled head and one silky shoulder. She appeared to be sleeping, and he decided not to wish her good-night. It was better for his peace of mind if he didn't disturb her now.

He fell into a fitful sleep, disrupted by dreams of running from a pack of howling wolves and sinking into quicksand in the arms of a very well-endowed young woman. He woke up somewhere close to dawn, and stayed awake until he heard Kristi stirring in the other bed.

He reached for his watch, and turned the face until he could make out the numbers in the darkness.

"What's the time?"

Kristi's sleepy voice did unspeakable things to his stomach. He shut his eyes tight, trying not to visualize her in the pajamas. "Six forty-five."

"Oh. Did you sleep well?"

"Fine. Did you?"

"Mmm, I think so. I had a weird dream, though."

"Yeah? What was it?"

"I don't know, it was all mixed up. I was with a lot of people, then they all turned into heifers and horses." She giggled. "Silly, isn't it?"

"I don't know. Some people reckon your dreams are trying to tell you something."

"I know. I can't imagine what turning people into horses is all about, though. Do you have weird dreams like that?"

He thought about the woman in the quicksand. "Yeah. Sometimes."

"Do you remember them?"

"Sometimes."

He heard the sheets rustling and knew by her voice she was stretching. "I hate sleeping in hotel beds. I never feel really rested in the morning. That's the nice thing about traveling in a camper. You always sleep in your own bed."

He almost groaned. These were the kinds of intimate things people talked about when they'd just spent the night together. All this talk of beds was beginning to stir up his body again. "Er...do you want to use the bathroom first?"

"I'm not in any hurry, if you want to go first."

"I'll make it fast." He slid his feet out of bed and felt for the jeans he'd shucked by the bed the night before. He stumbled across the room on bare feet, still tugging at the zipper of his jeans. He made it into the bathroom and closed the door. He had to come up with some way of ignoring her more feminine traits, he told himself, as he ran his razor over his jaw. If he didn't, he was in for some pretty uncomfortable days ahead.

With an effort, he put all thoughts of Kristi out of his mind and concentrated on what he would say to Sarah when they met. He'd been mildly surprised to hear she and Rory had stayed in town. He'd half expected them to have gone east. Rory had always bragged about how he would leave Promise and make it big in New York. Rory Madison had fancied himself as an actor in those days. Jed wondered what he was doing now.

As for Sarah, it was hard to imagine her married to that loudmouthed, arrogant bastard. Sarah was soft-spoken and sweet-natured. He'd never heard her say a harsh word about anybody, which was why it was so hard to figure out how she could have betrayed him the way she did. Well, all he could say was if she was married to Rory, then she'd got no more than she deserved.

He leaned forward and brushed his fingers across his jaw. He had to admit, he was curious about her now. She'd betrayed him, and destroyed his trust in women. He'd never again got close enough for a woman to make a fool of him the way Sarah Hammond had. Yet when he thought about her now, he could hardly remember what she looked like.

Well, if Kristi had her way, he thought, with just a touch of apprehension, he was about to be reminded. He wasn't sure how he felt about the prospect of seeing Sarah again. Right now he just hoped that Kristi was right about Sarah being able to shed some light on the night of the bank robbery, so that he could know for sure what had really happened.

He wasn't naive enough to think whatever she told him would clear his name. Rory was still a Madison, and apparently being an all-around rodeo champion with a fancy car and a high-class wife didn't make Jed Cullen any better thought of…at least in his family's eyes.

Well, that was one thing they couldn't take away from him. No matter what they thought about him, he was still a world champion. The best of the best. It should be enough, but it wasn't. He'd been dealt a huge injustice by the people of this town, and he wanted, more than he'd ever wanted anything, to put things right.

He managed to avoid ogling Kristi in her silky pajamas when she darted into the bathroom later. He waited impatiently for her to finish dressing, and had to admit when she finally emerged from the bathroom that it had been worth the wait.

She wore a close-fitting, dark red shirt with black trousers, and for once had left her hair loose. Tiny gold hearts dangled from her ears, and around her throat hung a slender gold chain. He still couldn't get used to seeing her wear makeup, and marveled again at the difference it made to her eyes. Kristi was a good-looking woman, and he couldn't imagine how he hadn't noticed that before. It seemed lately as if that was all he was noticing.

"Well, will I pass?"

She'd spoken lightly, but he'd heard the uncertainty in her voice, and hurried to reassure her. "You look every inch the society dame. You're gonna have every man out there panting for an introduction."

She sent him a look loaded with skepticism, but he could tell she was pleased by the compliment. "So, when do we talk to Sarah?"

"Right after breakfast. I thought we'd park in the town and walk down Main Street. There used to be a great little restaurant there that served the best pancakes you ever tasted."

She grinned. "I hope it's still there. Sounds as if you've got your mouth all ready for them."

It was on the tip of his tongue to tell her what he really had his mouth ready for, but he stopped himself just in time. A few days ago he wouldn't have thought twice about taunting her with one of his flip remarks.

Now the cute innuendos and provocative remarks would hold a grain of truth, and he couldn't afford to let Kristi know the effect she was having on him. She'd be out of there before he could blink an eye.

He didn't want that to happen. She was right, he needed her. He couldn't do this alone. Not while his family and maybe the whole town, too, still held a grudge.

He needed an ally, and he needed the air of respectability that being married gave him. In fact, he needed all the help he could get. And if he had to endure the torture of being around an attractive, sexy woman and pretending indifference, then he would do it. For right then, nothing in the world mattered to him as much as gaining back the respect that he deserved.

Chapter 6

Kristi settled herself on the luxurious leather seat of the sports car, anxious now to see the town where Jed grew up. It had been too dark last night to appreciate the scenery properly, and she was looking forward to walking down the same sidewalks he'd walked, visiting the same stores, eating in the same restaurant that served his favorite pancakes.

She wanted to learn as much about Jed Cullen as she could, because once this was over, she might never have the chance to know more about him. If she couldn't have him in her life, she could at least have the memories.

Jed drove slowly down the highway toward the main part of town, talking about his days in high school. The sun shone in a cloudless blue sky and warmed the interior of the car through the glass windows. Kristi stared out at the flat, arid landscape, and the smoky blue smudge of mountains in the distance. With the sunlight throwing a shimmering haze over the sandy soil of the desert, it looked like the heat of summer.

Jed parked the car in a public lot at one end of the street, and Kristi stepped out into the balmy sunshine.

''The restaurant's at the other end of the town. By the time we get there we should both have a roaring appetite.'' Jed told her, as they left the parking lot at a brisk pace. ''There's the library,'' he continued, nodding at a red brick building across the street. ''I spent a lot of time in there when I was a kid.''

At least that was one place that didn't have the Madison name stamped across it, Kristi thought. She tried to imagine Jed inside that ancient building, poring over books in the quiet shadows between the shelves. Somehow she just couldn't see him there. Jed belonged in the outdoors, his skin scorched by the sun and his lungs filled with the clean, fresh air of the prairies.

''What would you have done if you hadn't left to join the rodeo?'' she asked him, as they walked side by side past the store windows.

Jed glanced at her, seemingly surprised by the question. ''Heck, I don't know. All the time I was growing up all I could think about was horses. My pa couldn't afford riding lessons, but a buddy's father owned a few farm horses and I rode them until I got my first look at a couple of wild mustangs brought in by some Indians. I watched the wranglers break them, and it was the most exciting thing I'd ever seen in my entire life. From that moment on, I was hooked. I reckon if I hadn't joined the rodeo, I might have been out there working on a ranch somewhere, taming horses until the sun went down.''

Jed paused in front of a small restaurant. ''You hungry?''

Kristi nodded. ''Starving, as usual.''

Jed grinned. ''Never knew a woman who could tuck away as much food as you do and still keep her figure.''

Pleased and surprised by the comment, Kristi smiled back. ''Nervous energy.''

''Well, you got plenty of that, I reckon. Let's go try those pancakes now.''

The waitress was a stranger to Jed. When she found out that he was a rodeo champion and a former resident of the town, she made a big fuss over him, bringing extra syrup for his pancakes and hovering over him with the coffeepot until Kristi felt like telling her to leave them in peace.

Throughout it all, Jed seemed not to notice the waitress's attempts to be nice to him. He seemed preoccupied, and answered most of her comments with a vague nod. Even Kristi had a hard time getting any conversation out of him.

''Well, it looks as if you've made a hit with at least one person in town,'' she commented lightly as they left the restaurant a while later.

Jed grunted. ''If she'd known the whole story, she'd have more'n likely cut me dead. There are at least a half dozen people back there who know me well, yet they looked the other way as if they'd never seen me in their lives before.''

"Perhaps they didn't recognize you."

"They recognized me, all right. I'm the town criminal. How could they forget what I look like?"

There was such bitterness in his voice Kristi felt like going back and yelling at every one of those idiots who'd snubbed him. "They're wrong," she said fiercely. "And somehow we'll prove it."

"Yeah? Well, maybe now's our chance." He halted so abruptly she was several paces ahead of him before she realized he'd stopped.

She walked slowly back to him, wondering what new threat he was facing. He was staring past her down the street to where a sleek limousine sat parked at the curb. A young woman wearing a pale blue suit had just stepped out of the car and was about to enter the library Jed had pointed out earlier.

As Kristi watched, the woman glanced toward them, then paused, as if uncertain what to do next. Kristi's pulse skipped. She knew, even before Jed spoke, who the woman was.

"Okay, Cactus, put on your best act," he muttered. "You're about to meet Sarah Hammond—I mean Madison."

Kristi's nerves tightened as Jed draped an arm around her shoulders and began walking slowly with her toward the watchful woman. Her heart sank as she got her first good look at Sarah Madison. The woman's hair was dark blond, almost the same color as Kristi's, but she had light gold streaks that had been artfully put there by a hand other than nature. She wore it pinned up on her head in a look that was

designed to be casual, but must have taken ages to
achieve.

Although she wasn't beautiful, she was very attractive, with a flawless skin that would probably
have looked just as good without the carefully ap-
plied makeup she wore. Her eyes were gray, not
green as Kristi had imagined, and they were regard-
ing her with a shrewd expression that warned Kristi
to be on her guard.

"Jed," Sarah said brightly, as he paused in front
of her. "How absolutely wonderful to see you. I'd
heard you were in town."

Kristi wondered which of the town's gossips had
enjoyed giving her that news. She had to admit, the
woman was striking. Her well-cut suit fitted her slender figure to perfection, and the skirt was short
enough to reveal an appreciable length of silk-clad
thigh. Sarah Madison breathed elegance and upper-
class breeding. Now Kristi knew why Jed had been
so picky about her own appearance. And in spite of
the new clothes she wore, standing next to Sarah
Madison made Kristi feel as though the words Rodeo
Stock Handler were emblazoned on her forehead.

"Good to see you, Sarah." Jed looked as if he
wasn't sure what to say next.

Sarah turned to Kristi and gave her a warm smile.
"This must be your lovely wife."

Jed introduced them quickly, and Kristi held out
her hand. She would have given a great deal just then
to know what Jed was thinking. Pronouncing each
word carefully, she said, "So pleased to meet you,
Sarah. Jed has told me *so* much about you."

Sarah uttered a silvery laugh that sounded just a little strained. "Goodness, that must have been terribly boring. Not nearly as exciting as winning a rodeo championship." She looked back at Jed. "Congratulations, Jed. Your family must be proud of you."

Jed's expression seemed wary, as if he didn't quite believe what he'd heard. "You know the folks," he said cautiously. "Nothing much excites them."

"They must have been excited to meet your new bride." Sarah looked at Kristi. "So what do you think of our little town, Kristi?"

"I haven't seen much of it yet." Kristi slipped her hand inside Jed's elbow. "Jed and I were just starting on the tour, weren't we, honey?"

To her relief he picked up on his cue right away. "Sure thing, sweetheart." He patted her hand and grinned down at her. "Kristi hasn't had time to see much of it. We got kind of a late start this morning."

Kristi felt her cheeks warm at the subtle suggestion.

Sarah's gaze was intent on Jed's face. "I hope you'll be happy, Jed."

He nodded. "Thanks. Heard you got hitched to Rory."

"Yes." Sarah's voice went flat. "I'd have liked to invite you up to the house, but you know how Rory is."

Jed's expression didn't change. "Yeah, we weren't exactly on friendly terms the last time we met."

"I know. I'm afraid that was my fault." She

glanced at Kristi, as if she were afraid of saying too much.

"Jed told me about the fight," Kristi said, hugging Jed's arm closer to her body. "He's told me everything."

"I see." Sarah's gaze flicked back to Jed. "Well, you know Rory. He does get a little possessive at times."

"But you married him anyway," Jed said evenly.

"Yes," Sarah murmured, making no effort to hide the regret in her voice. "I did, didn't I?"

"So how is life with the Madisons? Any kids?"

Sarah shook her head. "No, unfortunately." She sighed. "It's strange, isn't it, how things never turn out the way you expect. Maybe if I hadn't been so quick to judge people when I was in high school, my life might have been very different."

Jed didn't seem to have any answer to that. Kristi wondered if she was overreacting, or if Sarah really was hinting that she'd made a mistake in choosing Rory over Jed.

"Well," Sarah said brightly, "I guess it's too late now. Perhaps it's just as well. Anyway, I really should be getting along. I have a few errands to run before lunch. Why don't we all get together for a drink, soon?"

Jed nodded. "Sounds good. I'll give you a call. We need to talk."

"All right. The Madison mansion. It's in the book." She lifted her hand in a brief farewell and ran lightly up the steps of the library.

"Well, that went better than I'd figured," Jed said brightly.

Kristi watched the elegant woman disappear through the door of the library. "She still has a case on you," she said quietly.

Jed laughed. "Yeah, I can just see Sarah Madison hankering after a rodeo cowboy."

He might laugh, Kristi thought, as she allowed him to lead her down the street, but Sarah's words echoed over and over in her head. *It's too late now. Maybe it's just as well.* That Jed was married? Is that what Sarah had meant? Kristi couldn't help wondering what Sarah would say if she knew that Jed wasn't married at all, and that it was only her own marriage that would prevent her from picking up where they'd left off that night sixteen years ago.

Jed didn't say much as they strolled past the small shops that lined the narrow street. She was surprised when he said suddenly, "I think we should pay my folks another visit. I want to ask my mother if she knows anything about that key. Maybe she can talk to pa and find out where it is."

"All right." She hesitated. "I thought you were going to ask Sarah what she knew about the robbery."

"I am. But I want to talk to my mom first. Anything I say to Sarah will carry more weight if I have that key in my hand."

"Do you think she knows who robbed the bank?"

He shrugged. "I don't know anything anymore. But if she does know, I'm sure as hell gonna find a way to get it out of her."

Kristi smiled. "I'm glad you're fighting back. It's time the people in this town knew the truth."

"Yeah, well, *we* have to prove it first, and that's not going to be so easy. The people in this town have always stood behind the Madisons. They'll keep their mouths shut tighter than a clam if they think we might have something on Rory Madison."

"Well, then, we'll just have to find a way to prove it," Kristi said stubbornly. "And we won't leave until we do."

She looked up to find Jed's warm gaze on her and her pulse quickened.

"You're some kind of woman, Kristi Ramsett," he said, with such tenderness in his voice she almost felt like crying.

"Aw, you know I'd do the same for anyone," she muttered, turning away before he could tell how much she treasured those few words.

She'd recovered her composure by the time they returned to the car, and eagerly agreed when Jed suggested he take her out to Coldstone Peak. She was curious about the place where Jed and Sarah had spent that fateful evening, though she wouldn't admit as much to Jed.

The highway they were on seemed to run straight into the desert, leaving all trace of buildings far behind. After a while Jed took a narrow, winding trail that led up the lower slopes of the mountains. Kristi had never been this far into the Arizona desert before, and she was fascinated to see small trees and flowering shrubs in the midst of the cacti. At a bend in the road a creek surprised her, tumbling and splashing between huge boulders, creating a little oasis among the patches of dry, dusty ground.

He took the next bend more slowly, then pulled off the road onto a dusty gravel trail. The tires crunched, raising a cloud of dust behind them as they crept along.

"Shut your eyes," Jed ordered, and she obediently did as he asked.

She felt the car halt, and heard the engine die.

"Now you can look."

She opened her eyes, and gasped at the scene spread out in front of her. The car was parked on the very edge of a sheer drop, so close she couldn't see where the ground ended and space began.

The clear air gave her a perfect view of the desert below, stretching out in all directions. To her right a pale ribbon of gray wandered toward a cluster of miniature buildings shimmering in the sunlight far in the distance. To her left the desert floor rose sharply to meet the smoky blue haze of the mountains. Right in front of her, far below, lay the town of Promise— a tiny scattering of buildings and houses that looked as if they been dropped there by a careless hand.

"On a clear night you can see the lights of Phoenix over there," Jed said, waving his hand at the distant town. "It looks real pretty in the dark."

"Oh, I just bet it does." Kristi pulled in a deep breath. It was as if she and Jed were totally alone in another world, far away from all the hassle and struggles of everyday life. Up there, with the wind rocking the car, it seemed as if nothing could touch them, and all their problems had been left behind.

She wouldn't let herself think about Jed and Sarah up there. That was another night. Another time. Right now these moments belonged to her, and she was going to enjoy every second of it.

"It's nice to know this is still the same," Jed murmured. "It's kind of peaceful up here. I used to come up here a lot when I was a kid."

"By yourself?"

She didn't know why she'd asked that, but she was glad when he answered.

"Yeah. I'd come up here now and again when I was fighting with my pa. It made me feel better, somehow. Cleared my head, I guess."

She glanced at him, sensing he needed to talk, but afraid of saying the wrong thing. "You didn't get along with your dad?"

Jed shrugged. "We didn't always see eye to eye on things, no. I guess we wanted different things. Pa wanted me to go to college. I wanted to quit school and work with horses. We'd go round and round about it, and end up with both of us spitting mad. That would upset Mom, and I'd feel bad. That's when I'd hightail it out of there and come up here."

She laid a sympathetic hand on his arm. "I'm sorry. I know what it is to fight with your father."

His sigh seemed to come from deep within him. "I felt guilty. I guess that was it. Pa had worked all his life in that refinery. His grandparents were immigrants, and his family were all hardworking blue-collar workers. He wanted something better for his kids. I was a big disappointment to him. Maybe that was why I had such a short fuse when I was a kid.

I felt like a failure because I couldn't do what my pa wanted me to do.''

"Oh, I know that feeling." She clasped her hands around her knees and gazed out at the magnificence of the desert. "No matter what you do, it isn't enough."

"Yeah, I reckon you do know."

She heard something in his voice and turned to look at him. His gaze was warm on her face, and her heart skipped a beat.

"We're two of a kind, I reckon," he said softly.

She smiled. "Maybe we are, at that."

He sat for so long she wondered quite desperately what he was thinking. She longed to ask him, yet was afraid of the answer. The last time he'd been in this spot, he'd been sitting next to Sarah. Making out with Sarah. Probably more than one time. How she longed to make out with him, too, and try to erase those memories with new ones.

"I guess if we're going to call on my folks, we'd better make a move," he said at last, breaking the spell.

She felt strangely reluctant to leave this enchanted spot, as if by doing so, she would lose the closeness she seemed to have achieved with Jed. "Can we stop in the town first? I'd like to take your mother a small gift."

He seemed surprised. "You don't have to do that."

"I know. But I want to."

He nodded, and she could tell he was pleased.

Once they were back in town, Kristi picked out a
tiny gold filigree butterfly pin for Jed's mom.

She was disconcerted when Jed followed her
around, wrapping his arms around her and dropping
hot kisses on her neck. She did her best to act as if
his behavior was normal, but by the time she'd paid
the storekeeper, who gave her a knowing wink, she
was thoroughly embarrassed. When she confronted
Jed about it outside, he gave her a wide grin.

"It was all part of the act, remember? By tomorrow the whole town will hear how I practically se-
duced you."

She curtailed the impulse to tell him he was over-
doing things. Jed's teasing was legendary. It was part
of his makeup, and anyone who wanted to be close
to him would just have to put up with it, and accept
it with good grace. She just hoped he wouldn't embarrass her like that in front of his parents. Though
somehow she couldn't imagine Jed relaxing enough
with his family to joke about anything in their presence.

The thought sobered her, and she was quiet on the
way to Partridge Creek.

Jed kept sending glances her way as he drove
down the highway. He hadn't meant to embarrass her
in the store. When she'd leaned into him the feel of
her firm breast against his arm had started up all
kinds of fires inside him. He'd figured the best way
to put them out was to make a joke of it all. He
should have known better than to tease her about

WELCOME TO THE
CASINO!
Try your luck at the Roulette Wheel ...
Play a hand of Twenty-One!

How to play:

1. Play the Roulette and Twenty-One scratch-off games, as instructed on the opposite page, to see that you are eligible for FREE BOOKS and a FREE GIFT!

2. Send back the card and you'll receive TWO brand-new Silhouette Intimate Moments® novels. These books have a cover price of $4.25 each in the U.S. and $4.75 each in Canada, but they are yours to keep absolutely free.

3. There's no catch. You're under no obligation to buy anything. We charge nothing — ZERO — for your first shipment. And you don't have to make any minimum number of purchases — not even one!

4. The fact is, thousands of readers enjoy receiving books by mail from the Silhouette Reader Service™ before they're available in stores. They like the convenience of home delivery, and they love our discount prices!

5. We hope that after receiving your free books you'll want to remain a subscriber. But the choice is yours — to continue or cancel, any time at all! So why not take us up on our invitation, with no risk of any kind. You'll be glad you did!

Play Twenty-One For This Exquisite Free Gift!

THIS SURPRISE
MYSTERY GIFT
WILL BE YOURS
FREE WHEN YOU PLAY
TWENTY-ONE

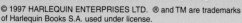

It's fun, and we're giving away *FREE GIFTS* to all players!

PLAY ROULETTE!

Scratch the silver to see that the ball has landed on 7 RED, making you eligible for TWO FREE romance novels!

5 20 7 11 26 9 0 2 16 21 18 31 8

PLAY TWENTY-ONE!

Scratch the silver to reveal a winning hand! Congratulations, you have Twenty-One. Return this card promptly and you'll receive a fabulous free mystery gift, along with your free books!

YES!

Please send me all the free Silhouette Intimate Moments® books and the gift for which I qualify! I understand that I am under no obligation to purchase any books, as explained on the back of this card.

Name: _____
(PLEASE PRINT)

Address: _____ Apt.#: _____

City: _____ State: _____ Zip: _____

The Silhouette Reader Service™ — Here's how it works:

Accepting your 2 free books and mystery gift places you under no obligation to buy anything. You may keep the books and gift and return the shipping statement marked "cancel." If you do not cancel, about a month later we'll send you 6 additional novels and bill you just $3.57 each in the U.S., or $3.96 each in Canada, plus 25¢ delivery per book and applicable taxes if any.* That's the complete price and — compared to the cover price of $4.25 in the U.S. and $4.75 in Canada — it's quite a bargain! You may cancel at any time, but if you choose to continue, every month we'll send you 6 more books, which you may either purchase at the discount price or return to us and cancel your subscription.

*Terms and prices subject to change without notice. Sales tax applicable in N.Y. Canadian residents will be charged applicable provincial taxes and GST.

If offer card is missing write to: Silhouette Reader Service, 3010 Walden Ave., P.O. Box 1867, Buffalo, NY 14240-9952

BUSINESS REPLY MAIL

FIRST-CLASS MAIL · PERMIT NO 717 · BUFFALO NY

POSTAGE WILL BE PAID BY ADDRESSEE

SILHOUETTE READER SERVICE
3010 WALDEN AVE
PO BOX 1867
BUFFALO NY 14240-9952

NO POSTAGE
NECESSARY
IF MAILED
IN THE
UNITED STATES

their pretense. He knew she was uncomfortable about it, especially with his parents.

Though he had to admit, he kind of enjoyed getting her riled up like that. He always had. Kristi Ramsett was a firebrand when roused, and he enjoyed watching her stand up for herself. She was spunky, and he liked that in a woman. It had been quite a revelation to see her standing next to Sarah Madison that morning. The two of them couldn't have been more different.

Sarah was cool elegance, whereas Kristi was spicy tomboy. Sarah was the kind of woman men liked to look at, but Kristi was the kind of woman men wanted to come home to. He'd be willing to bet that in a tight spot Sarah would wait for someone to rescue her, whereas Kristi would wade in and fight her own way out. More than once he'd seen her do it, and admired her for it.

It was a shame she wasn't married to someone who could appreciate her, Jed thought as he took the final bend that led to his old home. There were some who said that Kristi would never put up with a man in the house, that she was too fond of wearing the britches herself. But Jed had learned a lot about Kristi Ramsett in the last couple of days, and he had news for those guys. She was all woman. And he wanted in the worst way to find out if she was as much a spitfire in bed as she was when she was cornered.

And that surprised him more than anything.

His lighthearted mood vanished as he pulled up in the front of the house. His father wouldn't be home, he knew, he'd be at the refinery. But Wayne's pickup sat in the driveway. After the way his brother had hit on Kristi the night before, Jed wasn't too anxious to expose her to that again.

The door opened before he had a chance to ring the bell. Wayne leaned up against the doorjamb, his gaze raking up and down Kristi in a way that set Jed's teeth on edge.

"Well," Wayne said softly, "here comes the blushing bride. What have you two been up to?"

"You're a little too young to know that," Kristi said sweetly.

"Not much younger than you, I reckon."

"Really?" She raised her eyebrows. "Could have fooled me."

Wayne scowled, and Jed draped his arm around Kristi's shoulders and pulled her close. "Is Mom home?"

"Yep. She's fixing lunch. You got great timing."

"We didn't come for lunch," Jed said evenly. "I need to ask her something."

Wayne stood back and gave them a mock bow. "Enter, Oh Mighty Champion."

Jed pulled a face at Kristi and gave her a little push. "Go ahead, sweetheart."

She smiled at him, but her expression was solemn as she stepped in front of him inside the house. Once more he felt bad for getting her into this situation. She didn't belong in this backwoods town with its prejudices and small-minded beliefs. Neither did he. He didn't know why he'd even bothered to come back. He wasn't ever going to play in the same league as the Madisons, and he might as well accept it. He'd be better off leaving Promise for good, and putting all the ugly memories behind him.

But now it had become more than a personal issue. If people figured him for a loser, then they'd probably figure Kristi for one as well. They'd think her crazy for believing in a no-good punk who'd committed the first big crime in Promise and hadn't had the guts to stick around to face the music. He couldn't leave, knowing that Kristi's name had been tainted as well as his.

Besides, she believed in him, and if she was willing to stand by him, he owed it to her to fight back. He could only hope he wouldn't lose that fight, for if he did, he had a nasty feeling that he could take her down with him. And that was something he would never be able to outlive.

Chapter 7

Jed's mother seemed pleased to see him when he walked into the kitchen with Kristi. "You might as well stay for lunch," she said, laying places for them both at the dining room table. "It's only spaghetti, but it will hold you until dinner."

Kristi laid her purse on the small dinette table. "Can I help?"

Mrs. Cullen gave her a shy smile. "Thanks, but I can manage. Sit down and relax, and I'll have it on the table in a minute."

"Oh, before I forget." Kristi opened her purse and pulled out the small package from the gift shop. "I brought you something."

Jed's mother looked flustered. "For me? Oh, how nice. But you really shouldn't…"

"It's not much," Kristi assured her. "I just saw it and thought you might like it."

Mrs. Cullen took the package from her and opened it. "It's lovely," she exclaimed as she took out the pin. "Thank you so much."

"Here." Jed took the tiny butterfly and pinned it on his mother's blouse. He stood back. "Kristi was right. It's perfect. For a perfect lady."

Mrs. Cullen fingered the delicate pin and shook her head at him. "Oh, go on with you," she muttered. "Sit down before I start believing all that sweet talk."

Jed grinned at Kristi. "I told you she'd like it."

Reassured, Kristi sat down on the chair Jed pulled out for her. Maybe she'd misjudged Jed's mother, she thought, as the other woman turned back to the stove with a smile still hovering on her lips. Maybe Mrs. Cullen was intimidated by her new daughter-in-law, and that's why she'd seemed distant the night before.

Determined to put the other woman at ease, she said brightly, "Jed took me up to Coldstone Point this morning. It's beautiful up there."

Mrs. Cullen's smile faded. "Jed used to go up there a lot when he was young," she said quietly.

Dismayed that she might have said the wrong thing, Kristi edged over on her chair as Wayne slid onto the chair next to her, managing to push it closer as he did so. She saw Jed's warning scowl, and hoped the brothers wouldn't get into an argument at the table. The last thing she needed was to create tension between them and upset his mother. She was having a tough enough time getting the woman to warm up to her as it was.

Mrs. Cullen placed a steaming pot of spaghetti in the center of the table, next to a plate of sourdough bread. "You want a beer with that?" she asked Jed, and he nodded.

"Please."

"Me, too, Ma." Wayne nudged Kristi's arm. "How about you, gorgeous? You want a beer?"

Kristi ignored him. "I'd love a soda, Mrs. Cullen, if you have one."

"Oh, call me Martha, please." Jed's mother opened the fridge door and peered inside. "I can't have my daughter-in-law calling me 'Mrs. Cullen' all the time."

Kristi sent Jed a guilty look, but he was watching his mother. "I was wondering what happened to Dave Manetti," he said casually, as his mother handed him a beer. "Is he still in town?"

Wayne chuckled. "You bet he is. Dave is the mayor of our great town. Rory Madison takes care of his friends."

"Yeah, I reckon he does." Jed took a hunk of bread and bit into it. "I'd like to see him again, catch up on old times. You happen to know where he hangs out?"

Wayne narrowed his eyes. "I didn't know you were all that friendly with Rory's buddies."

Jed shrugged. "I wasn't, but it's nice to catch up on the old days, and I haven't seen too many of my friends in town."

"Tim Wilson's still here," Mrs. Cullen said, as she offered the plate of bread to Kristi. "He's the local vet. We used to take Ruff to him when he was alive.'' She sighed. "I really miss that dog."

Jed's mouth hardened. "I saw Tim this morning. He didn't seem to want to talk."

"Well, he's always in a hurry," Jed's mom said soothingly. "He's the only vet in town, so he's always busy."

"Too busy to stop and chat to an old friend he hasn't seen in sixteen years?" Jed threw a piece of bread into his mouth and chomped it down.

"He's probably put out because you didn't keep in touch with him. Or any of us, for that matter," his mother said, with just a touch of resentment in her tone.

"I didn't think you wanted to hear from me," Jed said quietly. "You all made it pretty clear you were ashamed of me."

"You're still our son, no matter what you've done."

"Or haven't done," Jed said grimly.

"Where do your folks live, Kristi?" Wayne asked, breaking the awkward pause that followed.

"Oregon." Feeling bad for Jed, Kristi sent him a sympathetic smile. He returned it, but she could tell he was doing his best to hide his bitterness.

"Do you have any brothers or sisters, Kristi?" Jed's mom asked. "We know so little about you. I wish we'd had more time to get acquainted." She didn't add *Before you married my son,* but the implication was clear.

Kristi gave her a warm smile. "My mother died when I was five, so there's just me and Dad."

Mrs. Cullen helped herself to spaghetti. "What does your father do?"

"He's a stock contractor for the rodeo," Kristi said, before she'd had time to think.

Jed's mom looked surprised. "Oh?"

Realizing that the other woman probably didn't know what that meant, Kristi tried to explain. "He raises livestock that are used in the rodeo—the horses and bulls that the cowboys ride, and the calves that the wranglers rope in the competition. He also used to produce rodeos, but he's retired from that. As a matter of fact, he's retiring period. He's putting the stockyards on the market."

Mrs. Cullen looked impressed. "Really. They make a big fuss of the rodeo here, but I've never gone to it. Too many people and too much noise for my liking."

"Rodeo pulls a lot of money into the town," Jed said, sounding defensive. "Promise wouldn't have half of these fancy buildings out there if it wasn't for rodeo."

"Or the Madisons' money," Wayne added slyly.

"Yeah, that, too." Jed dumped another heap of spaghetti on his plate.

"What made you take up working in a department store, Kristi?" Wayne asked, leaning toward her across the table. "You look more like the kind of woman who'd be happier working on a ranch somewhere. How come you didn't go work for your pa?"

"You never did tell me where I can find Dave," Jed cut in, before Kristi could answer.

Wayne sat back in his chair with a scowl. "Well,

I reckon you could find him at the community center. Gary runs the center and Dave's always there at the gym. I'd be careful if I was you, though. Rory's down there a lot, too.''

Jed grunted. ''Rory doesn't frighten me.''

''Maybe he should,'' Wayne said quietly. ''He's never forgotten you made a fool of him in front of everybody. As far as Rory Madison is concerned, Jed Cullen is a dirty name. You'd do well to stay out of his way.''

Jed's eyes glinted, but he ignored the warning and turned back to his mother. ''By the way, Mom, do you remember Luke Tucker coming to see pa?''

Martha Cullen nodded. ''Such a nice boy. Lives in California now, I believe.''

''Yeah, he does. Anyway, the key he gave Pa…it's important, Mom. I'd really like to have it.''

His mother's face grew stubborn. ''You'll have to ask Dan about that.''

''I did. You heard him. He won't talk about it. I was hoping you could find out what happened to the key.''

''You know your father. There's nothing in the world will budge him if he doesn't want to talk about something.''

Kristi saw the disappointment in Jed's eyes and her heart ached for him. ''I met Sarah this morning,'' she said, directing her comment at Mrs. Cullen. ''She seems very nice.''

Jed's mom nodded. ''She's a fine lady. Does a lot for this town. She helps out at the clinic, and runs all kinds of charity events to raise money for the poor families out in the desert."

"That's nice." Kristi finished the last of her spaghetti and laid her fork down on the plate. "It's sad that she doesn't have children. She must be lonely."

"I reckon she is lonely, all right," Wayne said, wiping a large hunk of bread around his plate. "Rory don't pay her no attention. When he's not at the refinery he's either at the gym or in a bar. No way to treat a wife, if you want my opinion."

"I don't think it's up to us to judge other people's behavior," Mrs. Cullen said tartly. "What other people do is their own business. It's family who matter, that's all."

Jed put his fork down with a clatter. "That was good, Ma. I hate to eat and run, but I promised Kristi I'd take her into Phoenix this afternoon, so we'd better get going."

Mrs. Cullen rose, picking up the empty plates as she did so. "You're always off in such a hurry," she grumbled. "I'd like to have more time to get to know my new daughter-in-law."

Kristi felt a warm glow at her words. She put an arm around Martha's frail shoulders and gave her a hug. "We'll stop by again soon, and next time we'll stay longer. That's a promise."

Mrs. Cullen's face brightened. "Come to dinner. Then you can talk to Dan, as well."

"We will." Kristi ignored the dark look Jed was directing at her. In spite of her disapproval of the way Jed's parents refused to believe in their son's innocence, she liked the older woman, and wanted to be her friend. She'd never had a mother in her life when she was growing up, she thought wistfully, as they left the house. It would have been nice to be part of this family.

"You didn't tell me you were going into Phoenix this afternoon," she said, as Jed pulled away from the house.

"We're not. I just said that to get out of there."

His voice sounded harsh and she peered up at him. "I'm sorry, that must have been hard for you."

"It wasn't easy. I had my hopes pinned on getting that key, and I don't like to keep being reminded of how I let the family down, and disgraced everybody."

"I'm sure they don't mean to make you feel that way," Kristi said uneasily. "They haven't seen you since it happened until now, it's bound to bring back the memories again."

"I wonder if it's worth the hassle," Jed said slowly. "Sometimes I think it might be better just to leave town again, and let them go on thinking what they want."

"Don't you dare talk like that, Jed Cullen." Kristi glared at him. "You can't just give up. Not only your family but these people in town are convinced you committed a crime. That's an injustice and it has to be put right. If you don't you'll never be able to hold your head up in Promise again and you'll carry that resentment in your heart for the rest of your life. This is your home, Jed. The only one you've got. If you don't have a home, then you have nothing."

He looked at her. "You won't have a home, either, if your father sells the stockyards."

The pain of it silenced her for a moment. "I guess I won't," she said slowly. "I'll have to start looking for another one."

As if realizing he'd upset her, Jed hurried to make amends. "Well, your pa hasn't sold the business yet. He might just change his mind when he's had time to think about it."

Kristi shook her head. "I think he's already thought about it. Once my father makes up his mind to do something, that's it. No one can change his mind."

"Not even his only daughter?"

"Especially not me. That's the price I've paid for not being born a boy."

His hand came out and covered hers. "Heck, I'm sorry, Cactus. I know it hurts."

"Yes, it does. And I know you're hurting, too. But at least you have a chance to do something about it. And I'm not going to let you leave until we've done it."

Something stirred inside her when he lifted her hand to his mouth and pressed his lips to her fingers. "You're good for me, Kristi Ramsett. Don't let me forget that."

She grinned, more happy than she dare say at his words. "I won't, don't you worry. So, if we're not going to Phoenix, where are we going?"

"I thought we'd pay a visit to that community center my brother keeps talking about."

She felt a stirring of apprehension. "What if Rory's there?"

Jed shrugged. "What if he is? I doubt he'd start anything he knows he can't finish. He's probably just as anxious to bury the past as I am. If I'm right and he did frame me, then he won't want all that dug up again. Someone might just find out the truth."

"Which is why he'll not be too happy if he sees you talking to his friends."

"True." Jed grinned. "But he won't be able to say too much without giving himself away. I reckon we've got him over a barrel, pretty much."

Kristi nodded, but she couldn't help wishing she felt as easy about the situation as Jed seemed to be feel.

The community center was a low, flat building with a red shake roof and beige stucco walls. Its archways and low outer walls reminded Kristi of a Spanish hacienda. Inside the spacious lobby an energetic-looking young woman sat a desk with a computer in front of her. She looked up as Jed and Kristi entered, and a flicker of recognition crossed her face.

"You must be Jed Cullen," she murmured, when Jed paused in front of the desk. "I've heard a lot about you."

"I just bet you have." Jed put his arm around Kristi and pulled her close. "And this is Kristi, my wife."

The girl touched a small container full of business cards with red-tipped fingers. "I'm Shelby Carruthers. I'm the assistant director of this center. Were you interested in joining the health club?"

Jed shook his head. "We're not going to be around long enough for that. We're looking for the mayor. Is he here, by any chance?"

Shelby raised her eyebrows. "Dave? No, he's not. I imagine he's at the refinery. He's the general manager there."

"He is?" Jed glanced down at Kristi. "Wonder why Wayne forgot to mention that." He looked back at Shelby. "What about Gary? Is he around?"

Shelby nodded. "That I can do. He's in the office down the hall. I'll let him know you're here."

"No, don't do that." Jed held up his hand. "We'd like to surprise him."

"Well," Shelby said doubtfully, "he doesn't really like people just barging in on him."

"He'll be happy to see me," Jed said, sounding confident. He started toward the hallway, pulling Kristi with him. "Gary is Rory's other partner in crime," he told her. "Maybe he'll feel like talking."

He found the door and rapped on it, opening it immediately without waiting for a summons, then ushered Kristi into the office and walked in behind her.

The man behind the desk looked up in surprise. He was a thin man, about Jed's age, except his hair was thinning and his droopy mustache gave him a despondent look. He wore steel-rimmed glasses that sat low on his nose, and he peered over the top of them as Jed paused in front of the desk.

"Hi, Gary," Jed said cheerfully, "long time no see."

"Jed Cullen," Gary said, sounding as if he'd just

swallowed a worm. "I'd heard you'd turned up like a bad penny."

Jed smiled without humor. "Meet Kristi Ram—I mean Cullen. My wife."

Gary Bolton gave Kristi a frank and somewhat arrogant appraisal. "Pleased to meet you," he murmured.

Jed nudged Kristi toward a leather armchair at the side of the desk, then perched himself on the edge of the desk itself. "So, how's life treating you, Gary? Doing pretty well for yourself by what I hear."

Gary shrugged. "Can't complain. The center keeps me busy, and the wife and kids take up most of my time at home."

Kristi watched the thin fingers playing with a pencil and wondered if Gary Bolton was nervous.

"Well, I won't take up too much of your time," Jed said pleasantly. "I was wondering if you could help me out on a small problem I'm having."

Gary looked up, his face wary. "Like what?"

"Well, I'm having a little trouble figuring out exactly what happened on that Halloween night sixteen years ago. You remember the night I'm talking about, don't you, Gary?"

Gary's brown eyes flickered from side to side behind the glasses. "Er...what night's that, Jed?"

"Heck, you gotta remember that night, Gary." Jed curled his hand into a fist and started thumping gently on the desk. "That was the night Boomer Carson got bumped on the head out on the highway and was robbed at gunpoint. The whole town was talking about it the next day, remember?"

Gary nodded, his gaze once more darting to the door. "I guess I do remember, yes. Vaguely. I mean, it was a long time ago."

Jed leaned forward. "Well. Let me freshen up your memory a little. You and Dave Manetti and Rory all went out together that night. Partied until after midnight, so I heard."

"Is that right?" Gary passed a hand across his brow as if he suddenly felt very warm. "If you say so."

"Well, that's what Rory said." Jed leaned in even closer, his face mere inches away from Gary. "What I want to know, Gary, is where the three of you had such a good time, seeing as how you didn't have any women along."

Gary leaned farther back and shook his head. "I don't remember. It was such a long time ago.... I'm not very good at remembering these things."

"Well, maybe I can remind you." Jed shifted his weight forward on the desk, bringing him even closer to the nervous man. "According to Rory, the three of you were riding motorbikes out in the desert. All by yourselves."

"Really?" Beads of sweat were visible on the man's forehead now. Kristi was beginning to feel sorry for him.

"Yeah, really." Jed's voice sounded lethal. "And I figure that the reason you don't remember is because Rory wasn't there that night. Or if he was, he left the party a good bit earlier than midnight, say around eleven or so. Or maybe you all left the desert around that time, and you were with Rory when he paid a visit to that gas station. Is that the way it happened?''

''No…of course not…I mean…we weren't anywhere near the gas station. We were all there in the desert until after twelve-thirty. Just like Rory said. We all went back to his place afterwards and had a beer. His father was there. He was mad at Rory for coming in so late on a school night, and told us to leave.''

''Uh-huh.'' Jed stared at him. ''I don't reckon you know what happened to the key of that gas station then.''

Gary began stammering. ''The key? What key?''

''Well, the way I heard it,'' Jed said slowly, ''was that Dave Manetti came across the key right after the robbery, and was holding it as insurance against Rory double-crossing him.''

Gary's eyes widened. ''That's crap. I never heard of no key, and nor did Dave. Nice try, Cullen, but you're not going to pin that ancient crime on Rory. Not after all these years. It's over and done with, so why don't you go back to riding horses or whatever it is you do.''

Jed leaned forward. ''You might have forgotten it, Bolton, but I can promise you I haven't. I reckon Dave will recognize that key when I show it to him. They can do amazing things in a crime lab nowadays. I reckon Rory's fingerprints, as well as Dave's, are all over that thing. I wonder what the crime for perjury is in this town?''

A dark red flush spread over Gary's face. ''Get out, Cullen. And don't come back.''

Jed smiled without humor as he straightened. "Oh, I'll be back. You can count on it." Holding out his hand to Kristi, he headed for the door. "Don't bother to show us out," he murmured, as the door closed behind them.

"That felt good," Jed said, when Kristi was once more sitting next to him in the car.

Kristi grinned. "All that stuff about fingerprints. Is that really true?"

"I doubt it." He pulled out onto the road and put his foot down hard on the accelerator. "But it gave Bolton something to think about."

"I think you really frightened that little man back there," she said, wondering if the mayor would be as easy to intimidate.

"Maybe. But by the way he was stuttering I'd say that he's a lot more scared of Rory Madison than he is of me. More than likely the only reason he's in that position is because Rory owes him. One wrong word out of Gary Bolton and he could lose that job."

"What about the other one? The mayor? Do you think he'll talk?"

"He might if I can dangle that key in front of his face." He gave her a wry grimace. "It's the big fish I'm gonna have to land if we're going to find out what really happened that night. And Rory Madison is going to be a lot tougher to deal with."

She looked at him with alarm. "You're going to see Rory now?"

"Nope. Not until I've talked to Dave Manetti. He never could watch his tongue. Just maybe he'll let something slip that I can use when I do corner Madison. But first I have to talk to Pa again and see if he still has that key. Before we do that, though, I reckon we should go back to the hotel and call Sarah. Maybe she can fill in some of the blanks.''

Kristi didn't answer him. She was too busy wondering how much Sarah knew, and how much she was willing to risk for the man she'd once loved long ago.

Betty May was behind the counter again when they entered the inn. When Jed caught sight of her, he immediately wound his arm around Kristi and pulled her close. She managed to laugh up at him as if sharing a private joke, and he dropped a brief kiss on her lips.

An elderly man standing at the counter watched them cross to the elevator, and Kristi held the provocative smile until they were safely hidden by the closed door. It was something of a relief when Jed dropped his arm and moved away from her to punch the button.

She was beginning to get very tired of the whole charade, she thought as the elevator rose swiftly to the third floor. It was hard being that close to Jed, holding his hand, feeling his arm around her hugging her close, exchanging warm smiles with him and suggestive comments, knowing all the time that he considered her more a kid sister than a wife.

Now and then she'd imagined she saw something more than friendship in his eyes, but deep down she knew it was just wishful thinking. She couldn't tell anymore what was real and what was part of the act.

It was ironic that she was doing her best to look and sound like Sarah Hammond, of all people. She was only too painfully aware that she was coming in a poor second. In more ways than one.

She wanted things to go back to the way they were. Before she'd agreed to this ridiculous pretense and come to Arizona with him. At least then she still had her hopes and dreams to hang on to. All she had now was the uncomfortable feeling that if Sarah decided to dump Rory, her next choice would be Jed. As for Jed, he'd be hard put to turn down the woman he'd left behind and never forgotten.

It looked as if all her hopes were buried, Kristi thought gloomily, and she might as well forget her fantasies. The sooner she realized that Jed could never be hers, the better it would be for everyone concerned.

She felt thoroughly depressed when they entered the hotel room. So far they had come up against a brick wall, and she was going through all this for nothing. She had told Jed not to give up, however, and she couldn't give up now, either. If she couldn't have his love, she could at least have the knowledge that she'd helped straighten out his life, and maybe then he'd be able to find some peace. It was small comfort, but it was better than worrying about him for the rest of her life.

She sat on the edge of the bed while he called Sarah. She'd thought of shutting herself up in the bathroom so she wouldn't have to listen to the conversation, but that might make her resentment just a little bit too obvious.

Jed seemed to wait for ever before he finally spoke into the phone. "It's Jed," he said, sounding a little unsure of himself. "I was wondering if we could meet tomorrow. There's something I need to talk to you about."

After another pause, he added, "I guess that will have to do, then. We'll see you then." He said good-bye and hung up. "She can't make it tomorrow," he said, walking over to the other side of the bed. "She's got meetings all day. We're going to meet her for breakfast the next day, in Phoenix."

"Oh, good," Kristi said, doing her best to sound enthusiastic. "I'm looking forward to seeing the city. I've never been there. Maybe I can do some Christmas shopping while I'm there."

He grinned at her. "I have an idea. Since we're dead in the water until the day after tomorrow, how would you like to go see a western shoot-out?"

She eyed him warily. "A show you mean?"

"Kind of. There's this place called Rawhide, just outside of Scottsdale. It's like a real Wild West town in the 1880s. It's got a few gift shops and every hour or so they have a gunfight in the street. It's kind of fun, if you haven't seen it before."

This time her smile was genuine. "It does sound like fun."

"Then we can go into Scottsdale in the afternoon, if you want. I reckon you could take care of that Christmas shopping there."

She nodded eagerly. "I'd love that. I've heard there's some good stores in Scottsdale."

"Okay, so where do you want to eat tonight?"

She thought about it for a moment. "Let's eat right here at the inn."

He looked at his watch. "I guess I'll jump in the shower and change my clothes. You want to go first?"

She shook her head, unsettled by the intimacy of their conversation. It was hard to sit there and look at him and not imagine him naked in the shower.

The newspaper that had been left outside their room that morning still lay on the dresser. She made an attempt to read it, but the sound of the shower intensified the image of his naked body, gleaming with soapy water, and she found it impossible to concentrate on the words.

She checked out her wardrobe instead, and decided to wear the black dress and the heels she'd bought for the awards banquet. She took the dress into the bathroom with her when it was her time to shower, and took her time preparing herself for the evening. She used a light dusting of makeup, smoothing out the remains of her tan.

When she came out, Jed was sprawled on the bed on his stomach, reading the newspaper. He looked up when she closed the door and whistled. "Hey, ma'am! Don't you have the wrong room?"

She wrinkled her nose at him. "Not funny. You've seen me in a dress before."

"Yeah, and I keep forgetting how good you look dressed like a real woman."

The words warmed her, until her treacherous mind wondered if he was thinking of Sarah when he'd mentioned a real woman. She had to stop this, she thought crossly. Petty jealousy wasn't her thing. She had to remember that she had no claims on Jed Cullen, and if he wasn't ready to settle for a meaningful relationship, that was the way the cards fell. She'd just have to accept that and get on with her life.

Trying to cover up her dejection she said gruffly, "Well, make the most of it, cowboy, because when this little trip is over, good old Kristi's gonna be back in her jeans."

His odd look was unreadable. "So you're going back to the rodeo, huh? You figuring on working for whoever buys the stockyard?'

She looked at him in dismay. For a while she'd forgotten that when she left Promise there'd probably be no job waiting for her, and no home either. "I don't think I'd be happy working for the business with someone else holding the reins," she said slowly.

"So what are you going to do?"

She shrugged. "I haven't given it much thought. Part of the reason I agreed to come to Promise with you was to give myself time to decide on my future. So far I've been too preoccupied to think about it. I might just leave the rodeo altogether, and find something else to do."

He was watching her carefully, and she felt uneasy. "Well, I reckon there's a lot you can do. Like being a buyer for a department store, for instance."

Her laugh sounded a little strained. "I guess that would make an honest woman of me, wouldn't it?"

His expression sobered. "I'm sorry, Kristi. I know how you must really hate telling all these tales."

"Well, it will be worth it if we can find out what really happened. Did Sarah ask you what you wanted to talk to her about?"

He shook his head, "Nope. She sounded happy I'd called her."

"I bet she was," Kristi murmured.

He grinned. "Jealous?"

"What? Of Sarah Madison? I don't think so." Kristi walked over to the dresser and pretended to sort out her purse. "I feel sorry for her. Married to that horrible man, no kids, and she's obviously not happy. It would be like being trapped in a place you have no hope of escaping from."

"Isn't that what most marriages are?" Jed rolled over and sat up. "I figure my mother must feel the same way. Stuck in a small town, going nowhere. She told me once she always wanted to travel, but Pa didn't like being away from home."

"That doesn't mean she's unhappy. No one gets everything they want. You just learn to accept that and go on. You play the cards you're dealt, I guess."

"Yeah, but sometimes you have to go out and fight to get what you want. If you accept things the way they are, you just might miss out on something you could have had if you'd tried a little harder."

She looked at him from under her lashes. "Good point."

He grinned. "I do make good sense sometimes." He glanced at his watch. "Your ready to eat?"

She nodded. "I'm hungry."

"Lady, I've never known a time when you weren't starving."

''Quit that, Cullen. I haven't exactly noticed you leaving food on your plate.''

''Ah...but then, I'm a man.''

''And that's a big fat excuse that covers just about anything. Whoever said this wasn't a man's world any longer was talking through his nose.''

''Well, I'll be the first to say that it would be a sad world without women.''

''Glad you realize that.''

She grinned at him. She'd missed their sparring. She'd missed being treated like one of the boys. When she was pretending to be someone else, kidding around with Jed hadn't seemed right, somehow. She couldn't imagine Sarah talking to him that way. She was much too sedate. It was so good when they were alone—she could forget about how she was walking and talking, and just be herself.

On the other hand, she had to admit she enjoyed his subtle comments and warm, loving glances. Even if they weren't for real. She sighed. Life just wasn't fair. Things were tough if she had to make pretend to be someone she wasn't to get a man like Jed's attention.

She followed Jed down to the restaurant, feeling a little self-conscious. The waiter who had served them before came hurrying forward and gave her a blinding smile. ''How nice to see you again,'' he murmured, as he led them to a corner booth. ''I do hope you are enjoying your visit?''

She thanked him, then gave Jed a suspicious look when she saw his grin.

"Looks like you made a conquest," he said, nodding his head in the direction of the waiter.

"Do you know him?"

He shook his head. "Never seen him before. There must be a lot of new people moving into the area." He looked around. "I can't see one familiar face in here tonight."

That should make things a little more relaxed, Kristi thought as she studied her menu by the light of the flickering candles.

"I don't know why you're bothering to look at that thing," Jed said, with the familiar teasing note in his voice. "We both know you're gonna order the steak."

"I might just surprise you tonight." She skimmed down the short list, irritated to see that there wasn't anything there she preferred to the filet mignon. She was tempted to order the salmon, just to contradict him, but thought better of it.

She looked up again to find his amused gaze on her face. As always, her heart gave a little skip. "So what are you going to have?"

"Same as you. The steak."

She scowled. "You don't have to sound so—" She broke off, her stomach sinking at the sight of the couple walking rapidly behind the waiter in their direction. "Well," she said unsteadily, "I guess there is at least one familiar face in here tonight. Sarah just walked in, on the arm of a very tough-looking man."

She watched Jed's face as he turned to look at the couple, but his expression gave nothing away. "I reckon this is as good a time as any for you to meet Rory Madison," he said, his voice deceptively calm.

Out of the corner of her eye Kristi studied the man walking at Sarah's side. He was a shade shorter than she was, though her high-heeled black pumps probably gave her the added height. He held her right arm above the elbow, with the possessive air of a man who dared anyone to touch her.

His dark hair was cut short, and black bushy eyebrows jutted over dark eyes. Rory Madison was at least twenty pounds overweight, and he had not aged as well as his wife, or the man who now sat watching him with pure hostility gleaming in his eyes.

Rory paused at their table, and gave Jed a cold glare. "Heard you were back in town. Still making trouble, I see."

Sarah looked at Kristi. "It's nice to see you again," she murmured.

Rory gave her a sharp look. "When did you two meet?"

"We bumped into each other in town this morning," Kristi said smoothly. She couldn't help noticing that Sarah's simple black dress screamed designer elegance. "It's nice to see you, too, Sarah. And it's a pleasure to meet you, Mr. Madison. I've heard a lot about you."

His eyes narrowed, though he gave Kristi a thin smile. "Pleasure's mine, Mrs. Cullen." His cold gaze flicked back to Jed. "Can't imagine what you see in this reprobate, though."

Jed's face darkened. "Maybe she knows an honest

man when she sees one," he said softly. "Which would let you out, Madison, wouldn't it?"

Rory Madison scowled.

"I really think we should get to our table," Sarah put in hastily. "The waiter's waiting for us."

Rory stared stonily at Jed for a moment longer. "Stay out of my business, Cullen," he muttered. "I'm warning you. If I have to, I'll ask the sheriff to keep you in line."

"Yeah, I guess he's on your payroll, too," Jed murmured.

Rory's mouth tightened. He gave Kristi a nod. "Hope you enjoy the rest of your visit, Mrs. Cullen. And for your sake, I hope you won't make it a long one."

He sauntered away, leaving Jed scowling after him. "Seems our friend, Gary, has been chatting about our little visit," he said darkly.

"Unpleasant man," Kristi muttered. "I can't imagine what someone like Sarah saw in him."

"Neither can I," Jed muttered darkly. "I'm surprised she's still with him."

There were a lot of women, Kristi thought, who would put up with a great deal for the sake of a nice home and money. She didn't voice her thoughts, aware that she was being catty. But her pleasure in the evening had completely disappeared, now that Sarah was sitting just a few feet away.

"Well," Jed said, as the waiter approached, "I reckon we should put on a big display to impress our friends over there. Guess you'll have to earn your keep again, sweetheart. Better order a drink. Just don't make it a beer.''

Kristi's heart sank. She wasn't sure if it was Sarah Jed wanted to impress, or her miserable husband. She only knew that the last thing she needed to do was pretend to be in love with Jed, and endure his make-believe love in return. But this was what she'd been hired to do, and she'd have to see it through for Jed's sake.

She ordered a glass of Chardonnay, while Jed ordered a Scotch. When the waiter disappeared to get their order, Jed reached across the table and took her hand in his, bringing it to his lips. ''You look sensational tonight, Kristi.''

''Thank you,'' she smiled fondly into his eyes, wishing he'd really meant that. ''So do you.''

''I'm a lucky man.'' He looked down at her hand and twisted the wedding ring around on her finger. ''I know they can't hear what we're saying, but I figure if we say the right things, they'll figure it out.''

Her spirits sank lower. ''Good plan.''

He looked up, and she saw his serious expression. ''What would you be doing now if you hadn't agreed to come to Promise with me?''

She pulled her hand away as the waiter approached with the drinks, and waited until after they'd given their dinner order before answering that question. ''I don't know what I'd be doing now, to be honest,'' she said, curling her fingers around her glass. ''I might have looked up one of my friends, I guess…though it's awkward this time of year. So many people have plans to spend Christmas with their families.''

He nodded. ''Don't give up on your father just yet,'' he said quietly. ''Family is important. Sometimes we have to accept a lot in order to keep things right between us and our parents.''

She felt sorry for him, knowing what he was going through right now with his own family. ''Once your family knows the truth,'' she said earnestly, ''they'll do everything they can to make up for those lost years. You'll see.''

''Maybe.'' He sighed. ''I guess I can't really blame them. I was such a rebel when I was a kid. I always figured the way to settle differences was with my fists. That didn't exactly cosy them up to me.''

''It's hard to believe you were so hot-tempered.''

He gave her a rueful smile. ''I reckon I still have that in me. I've just learned to control it better.''

''What about Wayne? Is he a fighter, too?''

Jed shook his head. ''Never was, as a kid. I don't know about now. Wayne was always a nervous kid, too scared of getting into trouble. My pa was pretty strict when we were growing up…and used his belt a few times to get his point across. On me, anyway. He only used it once on Wayne, as far as I remember. The experience must have really freaked Wayne out, and he was always so careful around my pa…though he was no angel. He got into his share of trouble, just like all kids do. He just made damn sure Pa never found out about it. I reckon Ma helped a little in that way.''

"Didn't your mother ever say anything when your father beat you?"

"I guess that was the way they'd both been disciplined as kids," Jed answered with a shrug. "It seemed the right way to them, I reckon."

"Well, all I know is that I could never stand by and watch my husband beat on my kids. He'd find himself out on the front lawn with all his possessions around him."

Jed grinned. "Yeah, I can just see you doing that, too."

"You bet I would."

She was unsettled when his expression grew serious. "You'd make a good mother, Kristi."

For a long moment she held his gaze, her heart aching for what might have been. Then she said lightly, "Maybe. But the way I'm going on now, by the time I decide to get hitched, it'll be too late to think about babies."

"That'd be a real shame."

She couldn't think of a thing to say. If only she could be sure that the warm look in his eyes was genuine, and that he did care about her just a little. From where she sat, she had a clear view of the Madisons' table. Sarah sat facing her, opposite her husband. She appeared to be looking in their direction, and some little demon prompted Kristi.

She softened her gaze, looked deep into Jed's eyes and deliberately mouthed the words, "I love you."

For a moment Jed looked startled, then apparently realized what she was doing. He reached for her hand, opened up her palm and pressed his lips to her sensitive skin.

A shower of sparks seemed to explode all over her body. Why this man, she thought miserably. Why, out of all the cowboys on the circuit, did she have to pick Jed Cullen to love?

The realization hit her. She snatched her hand back and pretended to be real interested in the Madisons' table. No, she couldn't be in love with him. Not Jed. Not when she knew how hopeless that would be. She stared in confusion at the lovely face of the woman at the table across the room. Why couldn't she be more like Sarah Madison? Maybe then she'd have stood a chance. Then again, she doubted if even Sarah could change Jed's mind about love. He was too scared of being caught in the trap.

That's what marriage was to Jed—a trap. All marriages were like that, he'd said. Stuck in a small town, going nowhere. Ever since she'd known him, she'd never seen him date a woman more than once. He'd never learned to trust…thanks to Sarah Madison. Yet still he worried about her, wanting to spare her the embarrassment of being caught up in Rory's nasty little scheme of revenge.

The food arrived, just then, sparing her any more agony. Jed seemed to take his time eating his meal, and Kristi wondered if he was trying to outstay Rory Madison. By the time he'd finished his coffee, however, the Madisons were still eating dessert.

To Kristi's relief, Jed paid the bill and left the table without another glance in Sarah's direction. At least the confrontation had been delayed for a while.

Jed draped his arm around her shoulders as they walked out, and Kristi could almost feel Sarah's gaze burning into her back. She might be fooling Jed's family with her masquerade, she thought miserably, but she was certain that Sarah wasn't taken in by it.

Jed was unusually quiet on the way back to their room, and Kristi would have given a lot to know what he was thinking about. She was still reeling from the shock of discovering she was in love with him, and was thankful for the excuse not to talk. She wondered how Jed would react if he knew. Probably put her on the first bus out of town, she thought gloomily. She would have her work cut out keeping her feelings hidden from him, especially if he insisted on keeping up the act.

What she should do was make up some excuse, pack up her things and get out of there before she got in any deeper. If there wasn't so much at stake, that's exactly what she would do. All she could do was hope that Sarah knew something that would help Jed clear his name. And was willing to talk about it. That wouldn't be easy if her husband was involved.

Kristi let out a long sigh. She couldn't bear the thought that they had gone through all this agony for nothing. Someone somewhere had to be willing to tell the truth. If not, she didn't give Jed much chance of ever coming to terms with his past and making peace with his family.

Jed lay on the bed, going over the evening's events while he waited for Kristi to free up the bathroom. He'd had his back to the Madison table, so he hadn't been able to watch them together, but from the brief moment they'd paused at his table he could tell that Sarah was unhappy. It was in her eyes, and the tense way she'd held her body when he and Rory were sparring.

He felt sorry for her, but then she could have easily left Rory. Her family had money, and it wasn't as if she would be on the street. Although she'd have to find a job to support herself, of course. He wondered what Sarah would do if she had to make a living. She wasn't like Kristi, who would have no trouble at all finding something else to do.

He thought about Kristi, being let down by her father like that. She was taking it pretty well, all things considered. But then Kristi was tough, and used to standing on her own feet. It was one of the things he admired about her.

He smiled, remembering her standing with her fists dug into her hips, mouthing off at him for some crack he'd made at her expense. His smile faded when another memory came hot on the heels of that one. The odd, tender moment when she'd looked across the table at him and mouthed, *I love you.*

His body stirred at the memory, and he rolled over in an effort to control the sudden surge of excitement. She had made it look so real. It was getting tougher to keep up this pretense. When they were in public they were behaving like typical newlyweds, cuddling and sweet-talking each other, just like regular honeymooners.

Everything they were doing was supposed to lead up to the happy couple rushing back to their hotel room to satisfy their natural urges. Only in his case that wasn't happening. His frustration was driving him crazy.

Every time he touched her, every time he kissed her, every time she looked at him with an invitation in those soft blue eyes, he longed to take her up on it. He spent most of his nights aching to cross those few inches between them and slip into bed beside her, and most of his days fighting his desire, forcing himself to keep his hands off her.

He wanted her so badly it was a constant ache in his gut, and there were times when he imagined that all he had to do was make a move and Kristi would meet him more than halfway. Many times he'd seen something in her eyes that had given him encouragement, only to have her shut him out the next second.

He couldn't take the chance of going through with it. She was playing a part, even if she was doing it really well, and he couldn't let himself forget that. She was a good friend. He didn't have too many of those, and he valued that friendship above everything else. He knew full well that if he followed through on his needs, he'd lose that friendship. Kristi was the kind of woman who wanted all or nothing. And he wasn't ready to give his all. Not to any woman. Maybe he never would be.

Kristi fell in love with the quaint little town of Rawhide with its tiny gift shops. The western storefronts looked authentic, and she was fascinated to-find local handcraft stores, as well as an old-fashioned ice-cream parlor and a real blacksmith.

Jed urged her to try her luck panning for fool's gold, and she joined the crowd around the "mine," swishing her pan in the water until she had a small pile of the glittering metal in the bottom. The smiling cowboy poured the minute amount into a miniature glass bottle and presented it to her with a flourish. She was thanking him when she heard the gunshots in the street.

"Come on," Jed urged her, taking her by the arm. "You won't want to miss this."

The gunfight began. Kristi watched the cowboys fall from the roofs of the buildings, and she shuddered as she realized one of them could really hurt himself. She breathed a huge sigh of relief when it was over and the "dead" cowboys leapt to their feet amid applause from the delighted audience.

Jed left her to browse among the shelves in the gift shop while he paid a visit to the men's room. While he was gone she bought a bolo tie with a bear's head in turquoise on a silver background, and thin, black laces finished with silver clasps. It would be her Christmas gift to him, she decided, and slipped it into her purse just as he came through the doorway.

"Ready for lunch?" he asked her, and she nodded. "Starving."

He laughed out loud, and the sound made her heart sing. "When are you not hungry?" he teased.

"Hardly ever." She grinned up at him. "My dad used to say my stomach was a bottomless pit."

He draped an arm around her shoulders. "Well, give me a woman who enjoys her food, that's what I say."

She loved the feel of his arm about her. She knew the gesture was becoming a habit. There was no one around to impress today. This moment was hers, and hers alone, and she was determined to enjoy it while she could.

They ate hot dogs and ice-cream sundaes for lunch, while Jed kept her amused telling her about some of his adventures with Cord and Denver.

"Denver and April's wedding is right after Christmas," Kristi said, as they left the ice cream parlor. "I hope we can find out something soon. I'd hate to miss that wedding."

Jed's smile faded. "Well, no matter what happens I reckon we'll make that wedding. I'd be in real trouble if I missed it."

"Denver would understand if he knew the reason you were here. I'm sure he would. And so would April." Without thinking, she slipped her hand in the crook of his elbow and gave his arm a reassuring squeeze. "Your friends would be the first ones to tell you to stay right here until you've cleared your name. And I intend to see that you do just that."

"We could be wasting our time. Even if I find the key there's no guarantee Dave will talk. And I'm damn sure Rory's not going to admit to armed robbery."

"I don't care," Kristi said fiercely. "We'll find proof somewhere, somehow. I just know it."

He looked at her and his eyes softened. "You

know something, Cactus, I'm real glad you're on my side.''

She managed a grin. "So am I," she said, with feeling.

Chapter 8

That afternoon Jed drove Kristi into Scottsdale. As they entered the town she was surprised to see the Western storefronts, which were strewn with brightly colored lights for Christmas. "They look almost as authentic as the ones in Rawhide," she remarked, as Jed pulled into a side street to park.

"That's because they are." He grinned at her as he slammed the car door. "Would you believe that cars are supposed to yield the right of way to horses here?"

She stared at him in delight. "You're kidding. Really?"

"Really," he assured her. "And if you stick around until January, you'll see the same gunfights on Main Street that you saw in Rawhide. They have this festival called Parada del Sol, when they celebrate the old West, and they have street dances and floats, and even a pony-express mail delivery to the post office.''

''That sounds like so much fun,'' Kristi said wistfully. ''I'd like to have seen that.''

''It's on every year…lasts about a month. Maybe you can come back sometime and see it.''

She smiled. ''Maybe. But right now I want to do some serious shopping.''

''Well, these are mostly souvenir and local craft shops here. If you want a mall we'll have to go up the street a ways.''

Kristi looked around at the windows crowded with everything from cowboy hats and boots to cacti in gaily painted pots and stunning pottery that made her think of beautifully decorated western homes—the kind she hoped to have some day, she realized. ''I think this is going to do just fine,'' she said happily. ''I know men aren't that crazy about shopping, so why don't I meet you back here at the car in a couple of hours? It will be faster if we shop on our own, and that should give us both enough time to get everything done.''

Jed looked relieved. ''Sounds like a plan to me.'' He took the spare key off his ring and gave it to her. ''See you in two hours.''

She waved goodbye then headed for the nearest store. Her shopping list was quickly filled and, loaded down with plastic bags, she was about to return to the car when a colorful poster caught her eye. It was pasted to the window of a small gift shop, and behind it picnic baskets had been carefully arranged, their contents peeking out on display. Brightly colored cloth napkins spilled over the sides of the baskets, in which bottles of wine had been placed, together with interesting-looking packages of food.

But it was the poster that held Kristi's attention. A couple sat on a bed, with a picnic basket between them. Plates of cheese, meats, raw vegetables and fruit spread out over the old-fashioned quilt. "You don't need a beach to have a picnic," the poster told her, and looking at the sumptuous meal the couple were enjoying, Kristi mentally agreed.

Studying the text at the bottom of the poster, she discovered that for a remarkably reasonable price, she could buy a picnic basket that promised to provide everything for a complete meal, like the one she was looking at.

The more she thought about the idea, the more she liked it. It would certainly make a change from eating at the restaurant in the inn, she decided. Plus it would give her a chance to pay for a meal, for once, since Jed insisted on picking up every bill.

Excited now at the thought of surprising him, she hurried inside. To her delight, Jed was nowhere in sight when she arrived back at the car, and she quickly packed her purchases into the trunk, taking care to cover up the basket with the other bags, just in case Jed should open up the back of the car.

He arrived just a few short moments later, carrying one small plastic bag, which he waved at her in the window. She watched him lay it in the back seat before settling himself down in front of the wheel.

"Is that all you managed to find in two hours?" she asked, as he started the engine.

He gave her a brief glance. "I hate shopping. I spent most of the time watching the football game on TV."

She sighed. "Men."

"I haven't bothered with Christmas gifts in the last sixteen years. I'm out of practice."

"You didn't buy gifts for Cord and Denver?"

"Nope. We didn't bother much with Christmas at all. We usually spent most of it in a tavern."

She nodded. "That's one way to avoid it."

"I reckon when you don't have family that's the easiest way to get through it."

She glanced at him, but he was looking straight ahead at the road. "Well," she said brightly, "you have family now. So you can celebrate it with the rest of us."

"Yeah, I reckon. Speaking of which, do you mind if we stop by my folks' house? I want to talk to my pa about that key."

"No, of course not." She hesitated. "Though I do think it might be better if you go alone. Your father might be more willing to talk to you about it if I'm not there."

He sent her a sideways glance. "You might be right, at that."

She was relieved that he hadn't given her an argument. The subject was bound to be painful, and Jed would be able to deal with it a lot easier if he wasn't worried about her feeling awkward. Besides, she told herself, it would give her time to prepare her bed picnic.

When they pulled up into his parents' driveway a

while later, he asked, "You sure you don't want to come in to see the folks? I reckon Ma will be disappointed you didn't stop by."

Kristi felt a small pang of regret. She would have enjoyed seeing Jed's mother. But Jed needed this time alone with his father, and she was anxious to prepare her picnic surprise for him. "Tell her I'll come by tomorrow and see her. There's something I really need to do back at the inn."

"Okay." He climbed out of the car and waited for her to slide into the driver's seat. "You be careful now."

"I will." She grinned up at him. "See you in an hour."

He gave her a long look, then touched the brim of his hat and walked around the car to hurry up the driveway.

She didn't wait for anyone to answer the door. She drove off, before his mother could insist that she come in with him. If things didn't go well for Jed, she told herself as she headed back to the hotel, he would need something to take his mind off his troubles.

After letting herself into the room, she laid her picnic basket on the bed, then quickly showered. The black ankle-length skirt she had bought in Las Vegas seemed ideal for the occasion, and she teamed it with a soft black-velvet blouse that dipped low in the front and covered her arms to her wrists.

She left her hair loose, and softened the effect further with gold earrings and a gold chain at her throat. A light spray of cologne sealed the image, and she

smiled in satisfaction at her reflection in the mirror.
Tonight she actually looked the part she was playing.

She squashed the inevitable longing for it all to be
real. That kind of wishful thinking was over. She
leaned forward to add a touch of lipstick to her
mouth, and started when the loud peal of the phone
disturbed the silence.

Jed's voice answered her breathless "Hello?"

"Don't worry about picking me up," he said, his
voice sounding gruff. "Wayne has some business to
take care of and he has to go right by the hotel. He'll
drop me off. I'll be there in a few minutes, then we
can go down to the restaurant to get something to
eat."

He hadn't mentioned his father and Kristi felt a
pang of apprehension as she replaced the receiver.
Jed had seemed a little depressed. It looked as though
he'd struck out with the key business. Now she was
determined to make him forget his problems for a
little while, and just have some fun. She smiled wistfully, remembering how they used to try and outdo
each other with wisecracks. It would be nice to get
that easygoing relationship back again.

After she'd spread all the food out on the bed, she
dumped the bottle of Chardonnay in the ice bucket,
turned the lights down low, then settled in to wait
for Jed. She was looking forward to seeing his expression when he saw the feast she'd laid out for him.
And if a good part of her anticipation had more to
do with how he'd react to her outfit than the food,
she refused to acknowledge it. She was not about to
let her regrets get in the way of this evening. She'd

simply have fun, she promised herself, and she'd quit obsessing about his indifference to her feminine charms.

"So how long are you planning to stay in Promise?" Wayne asked as he drove Jed back to the hotel.

"I guess I'll hang around until Christmas," Jed said, trying not to wince as his brother swung the pickup around the corner, practically on two wheels.

"Doesn't Kristi have to get back to work? I thought Christmas was the busiest time for department stores."

"Not for buyers," Jed said easily. "All their work is taken care of earlier in the season. By the time Christmas comes it's too late for the stores to stock up." He had no idea if that was true, but it sounded good. He was becoming an accomplished liar, he thought gloomily. Kristi was right. He'd come back to Promise to prove that everyone had been wrong about him, and that he was a respectable guy with a good life. But now it seemed all he did was lie to everyone. Not only that, he'd gotten Kristi into lying, too. He was just making everything worse for both of them.

"She's a good-looking woman," Wayne said as he pulled up in the parking lot of the hotel. "Somehow I never figured on you marrying someone like her, though."

Jed looked at him in surprise. "Someone like Kristi?"

"Yeah. I guess I always figured you'd end up with someone more like Sarah Madison. You know, the big money. You were so hung up on her when you were in school.''

Jed wondered how Kristi would feel if she knew her portrayal of an upper-class woman hadn't worked. It was an awful lot to expect of her, but personally he'd figured she was doing a great job. He would have been proud to show her off anywhere as his wife.

''Mind you, a woman like Sarah is a heck of a lot to keep up with. I reckon that kind of woman would be out of your league.''

''But not yours, huh?''

Wayne looked surprised. ''Me? What would I do with a woman like that? I've had enough problems with women to want to take on that kind of trouble.''

Jed gave him speculative look. Ever since he'd been back he'd had the feeling that Wayne was keeping a wall between the two of them. He was genuinely sad about that. The age difference when the two brothers were growing up had made it difficult for them to really get to know each other, but Jed had always loved Wayne, and there had been times when he'd gotten a few bruises defending his younger brother.

Maybe all Wayne needed was a little encouragement to bring down that wall. And Jed was willing to try anything to make up for the trouble he'd left behind when he'd lit out of Promise. He had no doubt that Wayne must have put up with a lot of heckling on his brother's account...and that was tough for a small boy to deal with. In a way Jed felt as if he'd abandoned his younger brother, and he really wanted to make amends for that.

Maybe, if he made an attempt to repair the gap caused by his long absence, Wayne would meet him halfway. It was worth a try. "Don't you have a steady girlfriend?" he asked, hoping Wayne wouldn't think he was prying.

He was pleased when his brother answered him readily. "Nah. After Nancy and I split up, I kind of lost interest in getting serious about anyone."

"I'm sorry. That must have been a bad time for you."

Wayne shrugged. "You get over it. It went bad from the start. Nancy didn't like me talking to other women, and I didn't like her telling me how to live my life." Wayne glanced at him. "How come you took so long to get married?"

Jed shifted uneasily in his seat. How he hated all this pretense. "I guess it took me that long to find the right woman."

Wayne sighed. "Yeah. I reckon the way I'm going, I'm never gonna meet the right woman."

"Why do you stay in this town, Wayne? There's a big world out there waiting for someone like you. Why waste your life in a little nowhere town like Promise? You could start a business in one of the bigger towns and make some real money. Make a good life for yourself."

Wayne shook his head. "I worked real hard to make it in this town. It was rough at first. No offense, Jed, but after you left, no one wanted to give me a chance. I was a Cullen, and that was bad news to some people in this town. I did jobs for free for a long time after I came back from college. I thought about leaving, but I wanted to make it here. I wasn't about to let anyone tell me where I could live and work. I'm proud of being a Cullen, and the Cullens have lived in this town almost as long as the Madisons. I wasn't gonna let anyone drive me out of town.''

"Like I did,'' Jed said quietly.

"You had good reason to go,'' Wayne muttered.

"No,'' Jed said heavily. "I should have stayed and fought back. I never realized till now how much my family suffered for what happened to me.''

"Well, all I know is, I couldn't be happy living in a big town.'' Wayne slowed to turn into the parking lot of the hotel, then brought the truck to a stop. "What about you? You never said where you're living now. You must have a home somewhere that you can go back to when the rodeo's over.''

Jed shook his head. "The rodeo's never over. I just keep going from town to town. My home is a camper.''

"Doesn't Kristi get tired of that?''

Jed caught himself just in time. "We haven't been married long enough to find out, I guess.''

"Not much of a life for a woman, I reckon. Always on the road, never settling down in one place. What about when she starts having your babies?''

Jed sucked in his breath. He felt as if Wayne had socked him in the belly. The idea of Kristi having his babies was so overwhelming he couldn't speak for several seconds. What was wrong with him, he wondered irritably. He didn't usually let stuff like that get to him. What was it about Kristi that remarks like that about her could make his insides turn to jelly?

"You okay?" Wayne asked, giving him a sideways glance. "She told Ma she wasn't pregnant. She wasn't lying, was she?"

"Not that I know of." Jed fought to keep his voice calm. "I guess we'll figure out all that stuff when it happens."

Wayne sighed. "Well, good luck. I know if it was me and I was lucky enough to find a woman like that who would love me the way Kristi loves you, I'd want a house somewhere where I could settle down with her and raise my kids, and I'd never look at another woman again."

Jed briefly closed his eyes. That actually sounded good, which was dangerous thinking. It was high time he put an end to this conversation. "Well, guess I'd better go take my wife to dinner." Apprehension tingled up his spine as he said the words. It was beginning to feel so natural to refer to her as his wife.

Wayne grinned at him. "Lucky bastard. Have fun."

Jed nodded grimly. "Yeah, I'll do my best." He climbed down from the cab, then watched in concern when the pickup hurtled out of the parking lot.

Wayne still had a lot of growing up to do, he thought, as he waited for the elevator to reach the ground floor. His flirting with Kristi was a good sign of that. Not that Jed could blame his brother. Wayne was right—Kristi Ramsett was a good-looking wom-

an. And sexy as hell. And if he'd had the slight-
est indication that he was gonna be so affected by
that, he'd never have asked her to come to Promise
with him. Because now he would have to spend yet
another night tortured by thoughts of what he'd like
to do to her, if only she'd been a different kind of
woman with a different set of morals.

Even now his body was heating up at the thought
of being alone with her in that room again. He had
to keep a tight control on his willpower, or he'd end
up destroying the best relationship he'd ever had with
a woman. He swore quietly. Why did things have to
get so damn complicated? Why couldn't he just enjoy Kristi for the fun person she was, instead of letting his animal instincts get in the way?

He reached the door and paused a moment to calm
his agitated thoughts before announcing his presence
with a sharp tap. He waited for a second or two, then
heard the lock click as she opened it.

The first thing he noticed was the darkened room,
and the dancing shadows on the walls, caused by
flickering candles placed on either side of the beds.
He saw objects strewn across the nearest bed, and
assumed it was the gifts she'd bought that afternoon.
But why was she examining them by candlelight?

Confused, he took his first good look at Kristi, and
his heart stopped. He had never seen her look more
appealing. Her blond hair framed her delicate face,
making her look utterly feminine. The black outfit
she wore hugged her body, and the long skirt was
slit to the thigh. He caught the glimpse of a long,

slim leg, and sucked in his breath. She was magnificent.

He stepped inside the room and closed the door behind him. She'd backed up and was standing close by the bed, looking at him with an uncertain expression on her face that tugged at his heart. The soft shadows cast by the candlelight fell across her face, and he was struck by the vulnerability in her soft, blue eyes.

He ached to take her in his arms and kiss away that defenseless look. He clenched his hands, willing himself not to reach out for her, to touch her hair, to run his hands over her body.

He knew she was waiting for him to comment, but his throat was dry and his head was spinning...and he couldn't for the life of him string two words together and make them sound natural.

The silence seemed to go on for ever, while he fought to regain his senses.

Then she lifted a hand and waved it at the bed. ''I hope you're hungry,'' she said, the words uttered in a strange, breathless voice.

His pulse leapt...and he almost groaned as his body hardened for her. Hungry? He was damn well consumed by the raging need he couldn't ignore. His blood felt as if it were on fire, and if she went on looking at him like that he was going to throw her down on the bed and tear off those tantalizing clothes.

He took a half step toward her and she spoke again, rapidly, as if afraid of what he might do. For an agonizing moment he fastened his hot gaze on her breasts, clearly outlined beneath the soft, smooth fabric of her blouse. Then he registered what she was saying.

"I bought the food this afternoon...I thought it would save us going down to the restaurant...and make a change from eating out. You've been so good about paying for the meals...I wanted to do it for once...I hope you like picnics...."

Her voice trailed off, and he dragged his gaze away from her delectable body and stared into her eyes. "Picnics?" he asked stupidly.

"A bed picnic." She threw her hand at the mess spread over the bed. "I saw it on this poster and thought it might be a good idea. Of course, if you'd rather eat downstairs, well, we can pack it up I guess...." Once more her voice trailed off while he continued to stare at her.

"I'm sorry," she said a last, when he still didn't speak. "I thought it was a good idea...."

Food. Of course. That's what she'd been talking about when she'd asked him if he was hungry. He could see it now...meats and cheese and some stuff in plastic tubs. With a supreme effort he pulled himself together. "Good idea? It's a great idea! Where did you get all this?"

She let out her breath, as if she'd been holding it for too long. "In the shopping center, this afternoon. They packed it all in a picnic basket and all I had to do was choose the wine." She pointed to the ice bucket standing on the bedside table. The long, green neck of a bottle protruded from the ice. "I got you some beer, too, just in case you didn't want wine. I just thought it would make a change from eating at the inn."

"I reckon you thought of everything." He was touched. It was the nicest thing anyone had ever done for him.

"I hope so. Will you open the wine?"

He noticed his hand was shaking when he pulled the bottle out of the ice bucket. He wasn't out of the woods yet, he warned himself. "I hope you remembered to get a corkscrew," he murmured. "These things are devils to get out with my teeth."

"Here." She held it up. "One corkscrew."

"You did think of everything."

"I can't take all the credit. Most of it came with the basket."

He looked down at the carefully laid out feast on the bed. "This looks real good."

"It does, and I'm starving."

For once he didn't laugh. He just kept looking at her, the wine still unopened in his hand. "You look real good, too."

He was alarmed when her face puckered up as if she were about to cry. He'd never seen her cry. He remembered once, when her favorite horse broke a leg and had to be shot, she got real close to it, but not one tear spilled out of those lovely eyes. She was a tough lady, all right. Only now she didn't look so tough, with that low-cut blouse, her hair all fluffed up and her cheeks glowing pink in the candlelight. She looked soft and feminine, and painfully appealing.

He dragged his gaze away from her, and concentrated on opening the wine. He was afraid if he kept looking at her, the throbbing need inside him would overpower his good sense.

Kristi watched him, intensely aware of the urgent fluttering of her pulse. She'd wanted to surprise him, and part of her had hoped he would be impressed by her appearance, but his reaction had surpassed her wildest dreams. She'd seen it in his eyes, and she'd heard it in his voice. For once he was really looking at her as if she were a desirable woman, and she wanted to hold on to this night, this fantastic moment in time, and never let it go.

Her body hummed with excitement. The air about her seemed to sizzle with it. She could sense the subtle vibrations between them, and she loved the feeling. She wanted to make the most of it, to play it for all it was worth, and to hell with the consequences. This night was hers, and she was damn well going to enjoy it. She knew she should ask him about the key, but she didn't want anything to spoil this magical mood she had created.

She watched him pour the wine into the plastic glasses she'd provided, then he carried them over to her and handed her one. He lifted his glass and touched it to hers. "To friendship."

She felt reckless, and heady with the approval she saw in his eyes. "To us," she said softly. She lifted the glass to her lips, and saw a flicker of awareness in his eyes before he raised his glass and drank.

"Good wine," he said, lowering the glass.

"Mmm. They gave me a taste before I bought it."

"Then I like your taste."

Her skin tingled. Everything he said seemed to have a double meaning. Or was that just her imagination?

"So," he murmured, gesturing at the food, "shall we get started?"

She nodded, and settled herself at the foot of the bed with her bare feet curled under her. She waited for him to get comfortable beside her, then handed him a plate. "Here. It's every one for themselves tonight."

"Yeah?" He grinned at her. "Sounds interesting."

Unsettled by the warmth in his eyes, she pointed out the various offerings.

"What's this?" he asked, holding up one of the tubs.

"Greek salad. It's got goat cheese in it."

He sniffed warily at it. "Smells okay."

"It tastes wonderful. Try it. Be adventurous."

He gave her a look from under his lashes. "Adventurous, huh?"

She leaned forward and helped herself to some ham and cheese. "You've got to eat something other than steak once in a while. Think of all that cholesterol."

He picked up a slice of cheese. "There's no cholesterol in this?"

She shrugged. "You know what I mean. Try the grapes, they're sweet and they're good for you."

He let out an exaggerated sigh. "If there's one thing I hate, it's a woman telling me what's good for me."

"Oh, okay. I'll just let you eat yourself into an early grave, then."

"I'd rather do that than exist on rabbit food." He stared at the salad in disgust.

"Oh, go on, taste it. You don't have to eat it all if you don't like it."

He speared a little of the salad with his plastic fork and touched it with the tip of his tongue, then took it all in his mouth. "It's edible," he admitted. "But it'll never replace steak and a loaded baked potato."

She shook her head. "You're impossible."

"So they tell me. Wanna beer?"

"I haven't finished my wine."

"Are you gonna tell me you prefer that to beer?"

She shrugged and took another sip of the wine. "I'm beginning to. It's a lot lighter and the taste is pretty good once you get used to it."

He narrowed his eyes. "Better watch out, Cactus. You're starting to take your acting seriously."

She glanced him, wondering why he'd sounded as if he wasn't happy about that. Or maybe he was upset about his meeting with his father. Deciding that she couldn't put off the subject any longer, she asked carefully, "So what happened about the key?"

His expression didn't change, and she couldn't tell anything from his voice when he answered. "I was coming to that. I guess the sight of you in that sexy outfit blew it right out of my mind."

Determined not to be put off this time, she asked, "Did your father tell you what happened to it?"

Jed sighed. "Yeah, he told me. He threw it out. When Luke gave it to him he thought he was just trying to cover for me. He was afraid the key would get me into more trouble, so he tossed it in the garbage.''

Kristi uttered a little cry of dismay. ''Oh, Jed, I'm so sorry. You were pinning all your hopes on finding that key.''

To her surprise his shoulders lifted in a shrug. ''Well, it was a long shot, at best. The good news is my pa is finally beginning to believe my story. He told me he had his doubts after Luke came back to see him, and then when I came back he figured I must have something to prove to come back to Promise and face all those people.''

For some ridiculous reason she felt like crying. ''I'm so happy for you, Jed. I know how much this means to you. Then it was worth coming back.''

''You bet it was. But I'm still gonna nail Rory Madison for all the misery he put my family through.''

She watched him eat another mouthful of salad and was pleased when he said, ''I'm surprised to hear myself say this, but this salad tastes real good.''

She grinned at him. ''See? What did I tell you? Live dangerously and you could be pleasantly surprised by what you discover.''

She was unnerved when he settled his gaze on her and murmured, ''Sweetheart, dangerous is my middle name.''

Flustered, she began gathering up the remains of their meal. ''I like to try out new foods now and again. I'll have to cook you one of my specialties sometime.''

"I didn't know you could cook," Jed said, sounding surprised.

"Well, I can't exactly make cordon bleu, but I've been known to turn out an interesting meal now and again." She leaned forward to retrieve the empty plates. "My father used to say that eating one of my home-cooked meals was like meeting someone for the first time. You never knew quite what to expect."

He grinned. "Sounds like you."

"Of course, I've been out of practice lately. When you live on your own you don't feel much like cooking. It's so much easier just to go across the street to a restaurant. But usually when I'm home with Dad I cook some fairly decent meals."

"Well, you are a lady full of surprises." Jed studied her with a thoughtful expression that quickened her heartbeat. "I never would have guessed that our tough little stock handler was domesticated."

She lifted her chin. "There's a lot you don't know about me, J. C. Just because I spend most of my time around heifers and horses doesn't mean I don't know how to run a house."

Jed grinned. "Don't let the rest of the boys know that, or they'll come knocking on your door for a free supper."

She looked down at the paper plates in her hand, feeling suddenly subdued. "I guess I won't be around anymore to cook suppers for them."

His teasing expression vanished. "Come on, Cactus, you can't really mean to give up the rodeo. Why, you belong there as much as I do. You wouldn't be happy unless you were wrestling an ornery heifer, or cussing out a smart-mouthed cowboy. That's your life, and I reckon you're stuck with it, just like me.''

She stared at him, all her happiness disappearing like smoke up a chimney. It didn't matter that she was wearing soft, feminine clothes, or had teased her hair until her arm ached, or that her perfume had cost a small fortune. All these past days of wearing shoes that pinched her feet, skirts that chilled her knees and makeup that clogged her skin and made her sneeze…all that fancy talking, and to him she was still just Kristi Ramsett, the stock handler. He was never going to see her as a real woman. Never.

She grabbed up the rest of the plates and slid off the bed. In her rush to get away from his penetrating gaze, she forgot about her long skirt. Her legs tangled up in the confining fabric and she sat down hard on the floor.

"Damn it to hell," she muttered, furiously gathering up the spilled plates.

Jed chuckled, and strode around the bottom of the bed. "Here, give me your hand."

"I can manage," she said crossly. She started to get up, got a foot tangled in the hem of her skirt and stumbled again.

This time he caught her under the arms and hauled her to her feet. "I reckon you'd better go back to wearing pants, Cactus, before you end up crippling yourself for life."

"I'm quite capable of wearing skirts if I want, Jed Cullen, and you have no call to make fun of me." She glared up at him, breathing fire.

"Aw, come on, Kristi, I'm not making fun of you. What are you so all-fired mad about?"

"I'm not mad. I'm just…oh, what's the point? You'll never understand."

As if realizing he'd upset her, he puller her closer. "Try me."

She looked up at him, fighting the ridiculous urge to cry. Of course she couldn't tell him. She'd die rather than tell him. She looked into his eyes, and her heart skipped a beat when she saw the sudden fire in them.

"Maybe this will help," he muttered, and lowered his head.

For a split second after she sensed he was going to kiss her, she resisted the urge to respond. For one split second. Then, as his mouth closed over hers, she wound her arms around his neck. She knew she'd been waiting for this, ever since he'd walked in the door. She also knew where they were going. She welcomed it…no, craved it, with every fiber of her being. Tonight was hers, and to hell with the consequences.

Chapter 9

This was like no kiss they'd ever exchanged before. This wasn't a brief touch of lips for the benefit of his parents and whoever else in town cared to watch. This was fire and chills, gentleness and aggression, tongue challenging tongue, passion igniting passion.

He still had hold of her under the arms. He moved his thumbs, brushing the sensitive sides of her breasts. Desire raced through her, robbing her of breath. She leaned into him, her excitement catching fire when she realized he was fully aroused.

"Kristi." Her name on his lips, whispered in the sudden stillness of the room, seemed to echo off the walls and resound in her ears like the roar of a stormy sea.

She forgot about the possibility of a broken heart, she forgot about Sarah and her presence is Jed's past. She forgot that she had no right to be in his arms, that this entire relationship was built on pretense and deceit. Tomorrow she would wake up to the cold reality. But that was tomorrow, and this was right now, this moment. This incredible, wonderful moment when passion hovered like a butterfly on the very edge of a petal, just waiting for the right time to move. And she wanted it with all her heart and soul.

She felt Jed's shoulders tense, and knew he was fighting his needs. "Kiss me," she whispered urgently. "Don't think, don't say anything. Just kiss me again."

"Oh, man, how I want you." The words were wrenched from him, as if he spoke against his will. He ran his hands down her body, cupping the curves of her behind and bringing her hips closer to him.

The hard pressure of his need for her twisted the desire deeper in her belly.

She wanted to touch him, all of him, every inch of him. She wanted to know his body as intimately as she knew her own. She dragged at the hem of his shirt and pulled it free from his jeans. His skin was warm beneath the shirt, the hairs soft and springy beneath her palms. She ran her hands across his chest and found his hard nubbly nipples.

He made a harsh sound deep in his throat, then buried his mouth in her neck. His tongue flicked over her sensitive skin as he traced a searing path down her throat to the low neckline of her blouse. She felt his breath, warm and moist on the curve of her breast, and she closed her eyes, anticipating the unbearably sensuous touch of his lips.

He slid his finger into the neckline and pulled the top away from her body, then slipped his hand inside to cup her in his roughened fingers. She shivered when his thumb brushed her taut nipple.

Desire gripped her, and she tilted her hips into him, the pressure building when his searching lips captured her mouth again. In all her wildest dreams she had never imagined the savage, hot craving that held her in its greedy grasp.

His hand stilled, and for a second or two she looked deep into his eyes. She saw torment and need, and a ravaging hunger that matched her own. Excitement drove her now, and she feverishly opened the buttons of his shirt. She dragged it off his shoulders, trapping his arms in the sleeves for a moment while she flicked her tongue across his nipple. She heard him suck in his breath and felt a surge of triumph.

"Kristi...are you sure?"

His urgent whisper fueled her passion. In answer, she slowly pulled off her top, then unfastened her skirt and let it fall to the floor.

His hot gaze moved over her body. "Man, you are beautiful. I never realized, never imagined..."

"So are you." She watched, her excitement mounting, as he unfastened his belt and pushed his jeans to the floor. His body was so strong, so vibrant, so very beautiful.

"Come here." Naked, he held out his hand to her and she moved closer, bathed in the warmth from his heated body. She trembled with anticipation, her thoughts scattering as he removed the rest of her clothes.

When she was naked too, he stepped back and slowly lowered his gaze from her face to her feet. Then he knelt in front of her and buried his mouth in the soft curve of her belly. She closed her eyes, and gently clasped his head with her hands, afraid that if she didn't hold on she'd collapse from the driving surge of pleasure.

This was what it was like to truly make love. This wasn't satisfying needs, or feeding curiosity. This was true mating, the union of man and woman, of lover and loved. And she loved this man. For good or bad, for always and ever, she loved this man. Even if he couldn't love her in return, she loved this man. And she would take whatever he offered this night, and hold it forever in her heart.

When he gently pushed her down on the bed, she went willingly, blindly, hungry for the release only he could give her. With his hands and his tongue he sent her on a spiraling path to the summit…and finally beyond, where at last she claimed the fulfillment she sought.

He would not let her rest, however, and joyfully she took the opportunity to explore his body, striving to give back the hot, sensual pleasure he'd given her. She must have succeeded. All at once his patience exploded, and with a hoarse cry he covered her with his body. "Now," he said fiercely. "I need you right now."

She waited while he expertly sheathed himself, impatient for the moment when she would feel him inside her. He raised himself above her, his breathing harsh and his eyes on fire. "Kristi..."

He paused and she smiled up at him, never more sure of anything in her life. "Now," she whispered back.

The coiling, tightening sensation gripped her again as he entered her. He found her hand and pushed it back above her head, entwining his fingers in hers. His undulating hips urged her into motion, and slowly she rocked with him, then faster and faster...until she was striving again, reaching for the pinnacle that would propel her into that incredible plateau of contentment.

One final urgent thrust of his body and they were there, together, spinning into space without thought or conscience. Together, as one. Together.

She knew that feeling couldn't last. Already it was slipping away as they lay side by side, with only the sound of their harsh breathing to disturb the silence. Neither one of them had mentioned the one word she longed to hear. She hadn't really expected him to say he loved her, but a tiny part of her had hoped, all the same.

She knew Jed's reputation. It wasn't as if she didn't know what she was doing. Still, it hurt. It hurt like hell. She felt like crying, but Kristi Ramsett never cried. Besides, she'd made the choice and no matter what happened, she would never regret having this night to remember. No one had ever made her feel so reckless and downright erotic. It was an incredible feeling, and even though she knew no one would ever make her feel that way again, she would never forget how it was to make love with Jed Cullen.

Jed lay awake for a long time after Kristi fell asleep. He'd done what he'd promised himself he'd never do. He'd lost his head and given in to his basic needs. It was all too easy to lie there with Kristi's warm body at his side, and forget about his convictions and just enjoy being with her. But he couldn't afford to do that. He couldn't allow what had happened tonight to cloud his judgment. Oh, it would be fun at first, and he had to admit, there was a certain, heady excitement in the thought of coming home every night to Kristi's warm, enticing body.

Tonight had been special, and he'd be the first one to admit that Kristi had a wild streak that could keep a man interested for a very long time. Any other man, that was. But not Jed Cullen. He knew where his path lay. He'd mapped it out a long time ago. He just wasn't cut out to be a family man. Sooner or later, he'd feel trapped, and start resenting Kristi for holding him down when he needed to be free. They'd end up hurting each other. Or worse, ignoring each other.

No, he needed the freedom of the open road, and the wide expanse of empty sky. He needed the variety of traveling from town to town, never knowing what was around the corner. He needed challenge in his life, flirting with danger to make him feel alive. What he didn't need was a woman tying him down. Even if she was as exciting, interesting and just plain fun to be with as Kristi Ramsett.

He woke up before her the next morning and slid out of bed, heading for the shower before she could wake up. He knew he was taking the coward's way out, but he couldn't bear to see the disappointment in her eyes when she realized that last night was the only night they'd be together like that.

He felt like a heel, but as he stood under the hot rush of water he assured himself that he was doing what was best for her. He was saving them both from a lot of heartache. It was better that Kristi understood right off the way things had to be. He could only hope that their friendship would survive, even though he knew he didn't deserve a woman like Kristi for a friend. Right then he wished with all his heart that he could have been different. For her sake. She deserved better.

Kristi knew, the moment she awakened, that her misgivings of the night before had been well-founded. Even so, it was hard to look into Jed's face when he emerged from the bathroom and see the smile that wasn't mirrored in his eyes.

"You're awake then," he said unnecessarily.

"Yes." She tied the belt of her robe securely about her waist. "Are you through with the bathroom?" Her throat ached with the effort to sound indifferent.

"Yeah. Look, Kristi, about last night…"

She couldn't bear to hear him say the words. She held up her hand in a sharp movement. "It's all right, Jed. I'm a big girl. I knew what I was doing. I'm not expecting you to make an honest woman of me, if that's what you're worried about.''

The relief on his face seemed to slice her heart in half. "I'm glad you feel that way. I guess we got carried away, what with the candles and the wine and the bed being right there...."

"Yeah...stupid, wasn't it?"

His expression changed. "I wouldn't call it stupid. It was a real special night, and I wouldn't take it back for anything in the world. I just didn't want to give you the wrong idea, that's all."

That's all, she thought bitterly. If he only knew how crazy she was about him. But he'd never know. She'd make damn sure of that. "Don't worry about it. Like the song says, it was just one of those things."

She walked past him into the bathroom, flinching when she caught the fragrance of his cologne. She'd never smell that cologne again without thinking about his naked body urgently rocking with hers.

She dressed carefully for their appointment with Sarah, conscious once more of the differences between her and Jed's former love. No matter what clothes Kristi wore, or how expertly she fixed her hair, she would never achieve that polished look that Sarah projected so effortlessly. Neither did she want to, she assured herself as she peered at her reflection in the mirror. She was heartily sick of trying to be something she wasn't. If it wasn't for this ridiculous charade she'd agreed to, she'd put on jeans and a shirt and to hell with trying to impress everyone.

Jed was unnaturally quiet on the way to Phoenix.

She didn't want to speculate on whether or not he was comparing her to Sarah. That would only make things more difficult when they met her for breakfast.

In an effort to banish the treacherous thoughts, she decided to find out more about his earlier relationship with Sarah Madison. "How long did you know Sarah before you left town?" she asked, as the car sped silently along the desert highway.

He sent her a sideways glance and she sensed that he was wary of answering. "About three years," he said reluctantly. "Her father was a lawyer in Phoenix, but they didn't like living in the city, so they bought a house in Promise and that's where Sarah and I went to school. It was the only school in town, where all the kids, grade school through high school, took their lessons. It was built by the Madisons right about the turn of the century."

"That must have been tough—all those different ages together. What about football? Did you have enough to get a team together?"

"We didn't have a full team, but our school played some of the Phoenix and Scottsdale teams. Didn't do real well, I reckon. Most of the kids were forced into playing for the sake of the school. I guess that was why I didn't take much interest in it. I wasn't about to be forced into doing anything I didn't have to do. I had enough of that at home."

In spite of the hard knot in her heart, she sympathized with him. Maybe it wasn't so tough to understand why he was the way he was. He'd had a rough childhood, harshly disciplined by a strict father who hadn't allowed him much freedom of choice, appar-

ently. Then he'd been unjustly accused of a crime
and his own family had failed to be there for him.
And the woman he'd loved. It was no wonder he
refused to take anything seriously.

He'd survived all that by adopting a careless attitude toward all the important things in life. Security,
a home and a loving relationship. If he turned his
back on all those things, then he had nothing to lose.
But he was turning his back on life itself. Everything
that made it worth living. He was depriving himself
of all the best in the world and accepting only the
dregs. And that was the real tragedy.

She was still brooding over these things when they
pulled up outside an elegant-looking restaurant that
seemed to have come straight out of the Colonial
South. Huge white pillars supported the wide porch,
and gleaming white steps led up to massive carved
doors.

Inside, it was every bit as luxurious. Eyeing the
plush blue carpet and crystal chandeliers, Kristi began to worry that her gabardine slacks and silk shirt
might not be appropriate for such sumptuous sur-
roundings.

"This is real classy," she muttered in an under-
tone, as a waiter in a black tuxedo escorted them
across the busy room.

Jed grinned at her. "That's Sarah. She always did
go first class."

Kristi bit back a sharp comment, aware she was
being petty again. Her mood did not improve when
she caught sight of Sarah waiting at a table by the
tall, narrow windows. Her blond hair was fashioned

into an elegant French twist, and she wore a colorful silk scarf artfully tied in a knot over the neckline of her obviously expensive cream wool dress.

"How good to see you both again," she said, as Kristi lowered herself into the chair that the waiter had pulled back for her. "I hope you have a good appetite. The food here is marvelous."

"If I know Kristi, she's starving," Jed said cheerfully, earning himself a murderous look from her. "She usually is."

"How very healthy," Sarah murmured.

Kristi gave her a tight smile.

"So how are you enjoying your trip?" Sarah directed the words at Kristi but her smile was for Jed.

"Lovely." Kristi picked up the menu and pretended to study it.

"I took Kristi to Rawhide yesterday," Jed said, sounding a little edgy.

"Oh, really? What fun."

Kristi uncharitably wondered what she was really thinking.

"I think I'm going to have pancakes," Jed announced, after a brief silence.

"Which kind?" Sarah leaned toward him to point at the menu. "They have so many to choose from."

Seeing their heads so close together, Kristi promptly lost her appetite. The waiter arrived at their table and hovered there, while she frantically searched the menu for something light. "I'll have the Continental," she said at last.

Sarah laughed. "That doesn't sound much like a person who's starving. Are you sure you wouldn't rather have Eggs Benedict? They are awfully good here.''

Kristi shook her head, and tried not to notice Jed's sharp look of concern. ''A sweet roll and coffee will be just fine.''

Sarah smiled at the waiter. ''I'll have the usual, thank you, Peter.''

The usual, Kristi thought caustically. She'd never even visited a hamburger joint often enough to order ''the usual.''

''Now,'' Sarah said, when the waiter had melted away, ''What was it you wanted to talk to me about?''

Jed looked uncomfortable, and glanced at Kristi. She gave him an encouraging nod.

''Well,'' he said slowly, ''I reckon I might as well come right out with it. I wanted to talk to you about what happened the night of the bank robbery.''

Kristi watched Sarah's face, but all she saw was surprise, and a look of bewilderment. ''I'm not sure what you mean.''

''Just tell me what you know about it.''

Sarah's gaze was perfectly steady on his face now. ''I know that the gun used in the robbery was found buried in your backyard, and that you were arrested.''

''You also know I didn't do it.'' Jed said levelly.

For a long moment Sarah stared into his eyes, while Kristi watched, her heart thumping unevenly against her ribs.

''Yes,'' Sarah said quietly, after a long pause. ''I think I do.''

"Do you know who did?"

She shook her head. "I'm sorry, Jed. I wish I did."

She'd sounded totally sincere, and Kristi was inclined to believe her. She glanced at Jed, and knew that he believed her, too.

"There's an awful lot of people in this town who think I'm guilty."

"It's easy to see why." Sarah laid a beautifully manicured hand on Jed's arm. "Jed, look at it from our point of view. The sheriff found the evidence in your backyard. You had no alibi. You'd been in trouble before."

"Kid stuff," Jed said sharply. "I'd never been in trouble with the law."

Sarah removed her hand. "In any case, you weren't convicted of the robbery. So why are you bringing it all up again now?"

"I might not have been convicted by the law," Jed said bitterly, "but I sure as hell was by the town. My family paid for that, and I owe it to them to set things straight."

"Then I guess you have to find out who buried that gun in your backyard." She looked worried. "Obviously whoever robbed that gas station wanted you to get the blame for the crime."

Jed nodded. "Uh-huh. Someone like your husband, for instance."

Sarah's eyes widened. "Rory? You can't be serious."

"I'm deadly serious." Jed leaned forward. "Rory was jealous as hell of our relationship. Not only that, he was pretty fired up about you dumping him for me. Didn't look good for his image...the big boy in town losing out to some hick like me.''

Sarah smiled. "You were many things, Jed Cullen, but you were never a hick. I always knew you were destined for great things and now look at you. All-around rodeo champion of the world.''

Kristi briefly closed her eyes as a dull ache settled around her heart. There was no mistaking that expression on Sarah's face. She'd seen it enough times on her own lately. Sarah might be married to the biggest man in town, but her heart still belonged to the man who'd left Promise as a boy and had come back a hero. Sarah Madison was still in love with Jed Cullen.

Kristi's pain deepened when Jed cleared his throat. He seemed bemused for a moment, as if recognizing for the first time what Kristi had suspected and feared all along. His voice sounded husky when he answered Sarah. "Yeah, well, it doesn't seem to count for much with anyone else around here.''

"It will," Sarah promised, "once we get this mess sorted out.''

Kristi winced. That "we" had sounded painfully intimate. It was as if Sarah and Jed were enclosed in a world of their own, and she was out in the cold looking at them through the image of some warm, translucent bubble.

"Tell me why you think it was Rory who buried the gun," Sarah added, as the waiter arrived with their meal.

Sarah's usual order was cereal and fruit, Kristi noticed. So that was how she kept her slim figure. She stared miserably at her sweet roll and wished she'd ordered the eggs Benedict.

Jed waited until the waiter was out of earshot before telling Sarah about Luke Tucker and the key. Sarah heard him out in silence then, when he'd finished, she sat back with a sigh.

"I wish I could say I was surprised," she said, with just a trace of bitterness, "but nothing that man does surprises me anymore. What does surprise me is that those two men were foolish enough to lie for him."

"What surprises me even more," Jed said quietly, "is why you married him in the first place."

Kristi's heart seemed to stop when she saw the strain on Sarah's face. She felt like an intruder on what had to be a painful situation. After all, these two people had been lovers, until Sarah had chosen to believe Jed guilty of armed robbery. She couldn't believe Jed had brought it up now.

Sarah stirred her fork in her fruit for a moment. "I was young and foolish," she said softly. "And I've paid for it. My life with Rory has been a living hell and filled with regret."

Kristi knew what she meant. Regret for letting Jed go. She glanced at him, wondering if he'd read the same message in Sarah's last comment.

His face was set in stone. "The creep," he muttered.

Sarah looked at him. "We have to see that Rory gets what he deserves. Somehow we have to prove he robbed that gas station and knocked that poor man unconscious. He could have killed Boomer.''

Jed nodded. ''I know. But proving it could be near impossible. Kristi and I have been working on it, but getting nowhere.''

''Well, at least your father is coming around,'' Sarah said warmly. ''That's worth something.'' She glanced at Kristi. ''You must be very upset by all this, Kristi. Not a very good introduction to our little town, I'm afraid.''

''It will be worth it if we can clear Jed's name.'' Kristi deliberately put emphasis on the ''we'' and smiled at Jed. Her pain eased a little when he put his arm around her and gave her shoulders a squeeze.

''Well,'' Sarah said heartily, ''let's think about what we can do. I suppose you've talked to Dave about the key?'' She speared a piece of melon and placed it delicately in her mouth, leaving Kristi to wonder how she could manage that so elegantly.

Jed shook his head. ''It didn't seem worth the effort without the key to back me up.''

''Hmm.'' Sarah frowned, the lines barely marring her face. ''Let me think. What about Boomer? Have you talked to him? Maybe he can tell you something helpful.''

Jed stared at her for what seemed an eternity to Kristi. ''Now why didn't I think of that?'' he murmured softly.

Sarah's laugh drifted across the table. ''No one can think of everything. I don't have Boomer's address, but I do know he's living right here in Phoenix. He shouldn't be too hard to find. The last I heard he was the service manager for an import car sales company.''

Jed turned to Kristi. "We should pay him a visit as long as we're here."

She nodded automatically. "Good idea." She wished she'd thought of it. It seemed so obvious now.

Sarah changed the subject then, and Kristi listened to her and Jed exchanging memories, laughing about people they knew, and felt more and more isolated. They shared so much in common, and it was obvious neither one of them had forgotten the time they'd shared together.

Remembering how it had been with Jed the night before, Kristi could hardly blame Sarah for clinging to the memories. She was quite sure that long after she had watched Jed Cullen walk out of her life, she, too, would keep the memory of him forever in her heart.

Finally they were ready to leave, and Sarah refused to let Jed pay the bill. "You can both repay me by coming to the Christmas pageant tonight," she told them, as the waiter took the check. "Seven-thirty at the community center."

Jed looked wary. "I don't think that would be a good idea. Me and Rory in the same room together could be bad news, especially if he's drinking."

Sarah sighed. "Well, yes, he does do a lot of that lately. But don't let him put you off coming. There are a lot of people who would be thrilled that Promise's first rodeo champion will be there. It will be good for your family. Especially Wayne. He's managing the sound system for us.''

Jed still hesitated, and Sarah leaned forward and patted his hand. ''Oh, do come. Show this town that you have nothing to be ashamed of, and that the Cullen name means something.''

''Well,'' Jed said slowly, as Kristi knew he would, ''if you put it that way.''

''Wonderful.'' Sarah smiled at Kristi. ''It will give the people of Promise a chance to meet your lovely wife.''

She just couldn't hate her, Kristi thought miserably, as she managed a bleak smile. Sarah's sincerity was hard to ignore, and it wasn't her fault if she was still in love with Jed. No one knew how easy it was to love Jed better than Kristi. ''I'll look forward to it,'' she told Sarah, hoping she sounded just as sincere.

She would just have to get used to the idea of Sarah and Jed together, she told herself as they left the table. Sooner or later Sarah would discover that he wasn't married. It surprised her that he hadn't told Sarah himself. Once she knew that Jed was free, Sarah would waste no time in divorcing Rory, Kristi was sure of that. It was just a matter of time.

Chapter 10

They all walked out of the restaurant together, then Sarah left in a flurry of goodbyes. "She's changed," Jed murmured, watching her hurry up the crowded street. "She seems tougher, and a lot less trusting than she used to be. I guess that's what life with Rory Madison has done to her."

"I guess." She was going to be a lot tougher herself, Kristi vowed. She'd always considered herself a strong person, but as far as her emotions went, she could still be hurt. And badly. She was beginning to realize how devastating life would be without Jed around to tease her, and keep her guessing with his provocative remarks. She would miss him dreadfully. She knew now why Jed had never been serious about a woman. He still belonged to Sarah.

It seemed that she was destined to lose everything

in one fell swoop. Jed, her job, her home…
everything.

It took only a matter of minutes to locate the car
dealers where Boomer now worked. "Boomer might
not be too anxious to talk to someone he thinks gave
him a concussion," Jed commented dryly, as they
parked a block away from the showroom.

Kristi made an effort to overcome her depression,
for Jed's sake. If there was one last thing she could
do for the man she loved, it was to help him clear
his name. "Why don't I talk to him," she suggested.
"He doesn't know who I am. He might talk more
freely to me."

Jed gave her a worried look. "I don't know if I
want you going in there alone. What reason would
you give him for asking questions about the robbery?"

She thought about it, while he continued to watch
her, his face creased in concern. "I guess I could
take the car in and ask him to look at it," she said
at last. "Then I could kind of lead up to it. He
doesn't have to know I went in there to ask him
questions."

Jed looked even more doubtful. "I'd rather go
with you. If he gets suspicious he could get mean."

Kristi laid her hand on his arm. "Jed, let me do
this, please. I can handle it…I promise you. If there's
one thing I know how to do, it's talk to people."

Jed's frown relaxed. "I reckon you do at that.
Okay, I guess it makes more sense. But if he starts
getting ornery, you leave."

She nodded. "I will."

He gave her another long look, then with a brief nod, climbed out of the car. "I'll be right outside," he told her, as she took his place behind the wheel. "Good luck, Cactus…and thanks."

She smiled up at him. "Don't thank me yet. He might not tell me anything useful."

"I'll still owe you for trying."

She shook her head, then backed out of the parking space. There was only one thing she wanted from Jed Cullen, and it was the last thing he was willing to give her. Putting her pain aside, she drove into the service bay of the dealership.

She waited half an hour in the waiting room until finally she was called to the desk. Boomer turned out to be a thin wiry man with a droopy mustache and sad brown eyes. When she explained about the "noises" coming from her engine he wrinkled his brow at her.

"Sounds like the fan belt to me," he said, rubbing the back of his neck. "I'd better take a look at it."

Kristi followed him out to the car, rehearsing her opening lines. She waited until he opened the hood of her car and started poking around inside before asking casually, "Didn't you use to work at that gas station out on the highway just outside Promise?"

He nodded without looking at her. "Yeah…a long time ago."

"I thought I recognized you. I used to call in there quite regularly. My aunt used to live in Promise."

"Yeah?" He flicked a disinterested glance at her. "What was her name?"

"Wilma Phillips," Kristi said promptly, picking a name out of thin air.

Boomer shook his head. "Don't recall no one by that name."

"Well, she didn't live there for very long. She was the one who told me to use that gas station. She kept telling me what a nice young man you were."

"Yeah?" This time Boomer's gaze rested longer on Kristi's face.

"Yes." Kristi gave him her best smile. "She was right."

A gleam appeared in the brown eyes. "Well, thank you, ma'am."

Kristi tilted her head on one side and looked at him from under her lashes. "I seem to remember her telling me that you got robbed out at that station once. That must have been terrifying."

Boomer straightened, obviously delighted at the chance to look heroic. "Nope, weren't nothing. Takes a lot more than that to scare me."

Kristi looked impressed. "Really. Didn't you end up in hospital?"

Boomer shrugged. "Just a little crack on the head."

"You didn't see who hit you?"

"Nope. Had my back to him. I was too busy talking to my girlfriend on the phone." He leered at her. "Used to be real popular with the girls back then."

"I can imagine," Kristi murmured. "Your girlfriend must have been frightened."

Again he shrugged. "Well, she didn't know what had happened until later. See, I was in the middle of talking to her, and I never even heard the door open. I looked up and saw the reflection of this guy in the window. He was wearing one of them Halloween masks, and the next thing I know I woke up in the hospital. Caroline said all she heard was the smack of the phone as it hit the desk, then it hung up. Reckon it was the robber who put it back. Good thing he did, seeing as how I wasn't supposed to be talking on the phone there after hours. Told the sheriff I was taking care of a customer's car, and that's why I was there late. Could've lost my job if word got out I was sweet-talking a girl when the station was supposed to be closed. Never did tell no one about that.''

"So you didn't really get a good look at the man who hit you?"

"Nope, couldn't tell nothing with that mask on his face.''

"And there was nothing about the man that seemed at all familiar? A gesture, maybe, or the way he walked?"

Boomer's gaze narrowed. "How come you're so all-fired interested in something that happened years ago? You're not trying to lose me my job, are you? 'Cause if you are—''

"No, no, of course not," Kristi said hurriedly. "I was just curious, that's all. Now what about my car? Is it the fan belt?"

Boomer stared at her for a moment longer, then started poking around at the engine again. "Can't see nothing wrong," he muttered. "Better start her up so's I can hear the engine."

"Well, I'm in kind of a hurry right now and I need

the car. I'll bring it back tomorrow and leave it here.'' She opened the door and hopped in.

Boomer slammed the hood down. ''You'll have to make an appointment.''

''I'll call.'' Quickly she started up the engine and backed out of the bay. As she drove away she saw Boomer reflected in the rearview mirror. He was scratching his head and staring after her.

She was relieved to see Jed standing at the curb waiting for her, but hated the moment when she had to tell him she'd learned nothing more from Boomer.

''Well, I guess that's that, then,'' Jed said gloomily, when she recounted her entire conversation with the service manager. ''We're plum out of witnesses now.''

''We'll think of something,'' she told him, but she had to agree, things didn't look very hopeful.

''I hope you're not expecting anything spectacular,'' Jed said to Kristi as they drove into town that night. ''The local people are not exactly polished professionals.''

She smiled. ''It wouldn't be a Christmas pageant if everyone was professional. That's what makes it fun, watching people you know having a good time.''

''Yeah, I guess.'' He glanced at her. ''I just hope they don't all crowd over to the opposite side of the room when I walk in.''

She sighed. ''It's Christmas, Jed. People are more tolerant and forgiving at this time of the year. You might be surprised.''

His mouth hardened. "Don't bet on it."

She felt nervous as they parked behind the community center and walked across the parking lot behind a group of laughing, chattering people. As they approached the door she saw a woman nudge her companion, drawing his attention to them. Neither one of them seemed too thrilled to see Jed.

Kristi's nerves tightened when she saw the looks sent their way as they entered the center. No one seemed inclined to be friendly toward them. She was beginning to think that Jed had been right. It had been a big mistake to think he could wipe out their image of him as an armed thug.

Kristi left her jacket with the coatroom attendant, then she walked with Jed to a huge room where chairs had been set up in front of a small stage. As the pageant began, she did her best to ignore the tense atmosphere around her and enjoy the Christmas play. She recognized Shelby, who had a walk-on part, and Betty May, the receptionist from the hotel, who's shrill voice overwhelmed everyone else on stage. The children were adorable however, and Kristi managed to forget her worries and even laughed at the earnest performances of the little ones.

At last the curtains drew together and the cast appeared to make their final bows. The applause died down, and Kristi felt a stab of apprehension as Rory Madison walked out onto the stage. His gaze seemed to be boring right into Jed as he spoke into the microphone, though Kristi knew he probably couldn't see them sitting back there in the dark.

Rory thanked everyone for coming to the pageant,

then announced that light refreshments would be served in the next room, while the chairs were being cleared away to make room for dancing. A bar had been set up at the rear of the room, Rory added, amidst quiet cheers, for those who enjoyed a more potent refreshment.

Judging from Rory's slurred speech and somewhat unsteady gait as he walked offstage it was obvious to Kristi that he'd already sampled refreshments from the bar. The knowledge didn't lessen her uneasiness.

The man was evil. She could just imagine him hitting poor Boomer on the head then calmly replacing the phone.

"Well," Jed said heavily as he rose from his seat, "I reckon we made our point. Let's go pay our respects to Sarah and then hightail it out of here. I'm not in the mood for refreshments."

"I just saw her go into the other room," Kristi said, standing up with him. "Rory wasn't with her."

"Probably gone back to the bar," Jed muttered. He took hold of Kristi's arm and steered her past the people standing in the aisle.

They reached the last row and were just about to turn the corner when a stocky figure stepped in front of Jed and barred his way. "Where do you think you're going, Cullen?" Rory asked unpleasantly. "Don't you know you're unwelcome here?"

"I'm going to thank your wife for inviting us," Jed said evenly. "And then I'll be more than happy to get out of here."

Rory shook his head. "You're not going near my

wife, Cullen. You've caused more than enough trouble for her. You're not going anywhere near her.''

"And you think you're man enough to stop me?"

Rory's sneer contorted his face. "You can bet on it."

"I don't think so."

Jed made a move to push past him, but Rory shifted his weight to block him again. "I said beat it, Cullen. You're nothing but a low-down thief and a liar, and I don't want my wife associating with a bum like you."

Jed nodded, and Kristi felt chilled by the cold, murderous look on his face. "A thief and a liar. Well, you should know all about that, Madison, since it was you who robbed that gas station on Halloween and then tried to put the blame on me."

Rory let out an exaggerated sigh. "Not that old story again."

"Yeah, that old story again. Only this time I'm not running away. This time I'm going to make sure everyone knows what really happened."

Rory shook his head. "No one believed you all those years ago, Cullen, and they're sure as hell not going to believe you now."

Jed smiled—a thin, mirthless stretch of his lips. "No? I wouldn't be so sure about that. You might have bought off Dave and Gary, Madison, but there's one person you forgot."

Watching Rory's face, Kristi saw a flicker of doubt in his dark eyes. She had no idea what Jed was getting at, other than a massive bluff, but there was no doubt he had Rory worried.

"If you're talking about my wife, Cullen—"

"I'm not talking about Sarah. You made sure she knew nothing about what really happened. I'm talking about Boomer Carson, Rory. I talked to him today and he had some interesting things to say."

Rory's face went white. "Oh, yeah? Well, anything he says is a bald-faced lie."

"You didn't think the gas station would be open when you got there, did you, Rory?" Jed said grimly. "You just planned on breaking a window and making it look like a robbery. Only when you got there, Boomer was still in the office, and you had to hit him before he recognized you. Boomer was too afraid to say much about it back then, but he wasn't afraid to talk to me today."

"Boomer never saw who hit him," Rory said nervously. "He was too busy talking to his girlfriend on the phone."

Kristi caught her breath. Now she knew what Jed was doing…and it had worked.

"And just how did you happen to know about that?" Jed asked quietly.

Rory sent a wild look around him, as if he'd just realized he'd been cornered. "Boomer told me…he told everyone later."

"No, he didn't," Kristi said firmly. "He told me he never told anyone about that, in case he lost his job. The only person besides Jed and myself who could have known that Boomer was talking to his girlfriend was the robber."

Rory's black gaze shifted to Kristi, and the look

in his eyes scared her. "And you can just keep your dirty little nose out of it and shut your mouth."

He grunted as Jed took a fistful of his shirt. "No one talks to my wife that way, Madison. Not even you."

Rory placed two hands on Jed's chest and shoved him away.

Kristi looked around at the gathering crowd and tugged on Jed's sleeve. "Let it go, Jed. Half these people here heard Rory admit he knew about Boomer's phone call. It's enough, Jed. They know he was lying. That's all you wanted."

"No," Jed muttered. "It's not all I want. All these years, all the shame put on my family, driving me out of town...no, I want more."

Rory managed a sickly sounding laugh. "Forget it, Cullen. You were always a loser and you always will be...and no shiny little buckle on your belt is going to make any difference. These people know and respect me, and no one's going to care about something that happened all those years ago, so quit whining about it and go back to that fleapit where you belong."

Kristi jumped as Jed let out a growl. His fist shot out and landed with a sickening thud on Rory's jaw. For a moment Rory's eyes glazed over and his knees buckled, but then he recovered himself, shook his head and charged at Jed like an angry bull.

"Stop them," Kristi cried out, looking around for Wayne, or anyone else who might put an end to what was now a raging battle between the two men.

"Someone call the sheriff," a voice called out, as people scrambled out of the way of the flailing fists.

"No!" Kristi cried, "That's not necessary. Someone please stop them." She looked around, unable to believe no one would step in between the two men.

Then, to her relief, she saw Wayne push his way through the crowd. "What the hell?" he said, as he reached Kristi's side.

Just then Jed let fly a punch that almost lifted Rory off his feet. This time he went down and stayed down. That's when Kristi saw Sarah. She was standing on the other side of the room with such a look of agony on her face, Kristi felt bad for her.

Jed looked at his fist and shook it, then glanced at Kristi. She almost cried out again when she saw the blood on him. Before she could say anything Sarah darted over to them. At first Kristi thought she was going to help Rory, who was trying to sit up. But Sarah ignored her husband and put her hand on Jed's arm.

"Oh, Jed, your poor face. Are you all right?"

"I'm fine," Jed said gruffly. He seemed to notice the spectators for the first time, and lifted his hands. "I'm sorry. But he had it coming."

"You're a fool, Jed," Wayne said gruffly. "Rory won't let you get away with this."

Jed just looked at him...such a lost look it broke Kristi's heart.

A stirring among the people near the door turned her head, and the sight of the sheriff striding toward them caused her spirits to sink even more. Now Jed was in real trouble. She looked down at Rory, who was sitting up, nursing a split lip.

He looked up as the sheriff spoke. "Thank God you're here," he muttered thickly. "The jerk was going to kill me."

Kristi let out a cry of protest, but Jed shook his head at her. *Stay out of it,* he silently mouthed at her.

The sheriff looked at the people crowded around them. "Anyone here want to tell me what happened?"

Some of them shook their heads. The rest just melted away and disappeared.

"Whatever happened," Sarah said earnestly, "I'm sure Rory deserved it."

"You bet he did," Wayne put in.

"Will you be pressing charges, Mr. Madison?" the sheriff asked, ignoring them both.

A thin stream of blood trickled from Rory's lip as he staggered to his feet. He glared at Jed. "You bet I'm pressing charges. Assault and battery. Attempted murder. Whatever it takes to put him in jail."

"You need a lawyer," Kristi said urgently. "I'll get you one."

Jed looked at her, and the cold, hard expression in his eyes frightened her.

The sheriff took out a notebook and flipped it open. "Name?"

"Cullen," Jed said quietly. "Jed Cullen."

The other man nodded. "Oh, yeah, I know who you are. You'd better come with me. Reckon a night in jail will cool you off some."

"You can't do that," Kristi protested. "I demand that you let him talk to a lawyer first."

The sheriff looked at her with cold blue eyes. "And who might you be?"

She opened her mouth, then shut it again. It was one thing to lie to the people of Promise about being married to Jed, but quite another to lie to a law officer.

"Don't worry, Jed," Sarah said, laying a reassuring hand on his arm again. "I'll talk to my lawyer in the morning." She gave Rory a cold glance. "The same one who'll be handling my divorce."

Kristi felt a wave of despair.

Rory opened his mouth, then shut it again. He sent Jed one last, ferocious glare, then stalked over to the door and disappeared.

The rest of the onlookers drifted away now that the excitement was over.

The sheriff took hold of Jed's arm. "If you come quietly I won't have to cuff you."

"I'll come quietly," Jed said grimly. He looked at Sarah, who smiled up at him.

"I'll see you in the morning," she said. "With my lawyer."

"Thanks." He looked at Kristi then, and she could see it in his eyes. She braced herself for the words she knew were coming.

"Go back to Las Vegas, Kristi, and try to forget you were ever in Promise, Arizona."

She had been prepared for it. She just hadn't expected it to hurt so much. "I can't leave you like this, Jed. I have to know you'll be all right."

"I'll be fine." He sounded immeasurably sad and her throat ached with the effort to hold back the tears. "So go back to Las Vegas. You can take the car and leave it by my camper." He looked at Wayne. "You can run me up there when this is over."

He didn't have to tell her. Her job was over. "Would you like me to call Cord or Denver?"

"No. For God's sake, Kristi, don't call anyone or tell anyone anything. Just forget about this. Forget about me. Pretend it never happened. Just go back and get on with your life, okay?"

Her pride came to the rescue, and she lifted her chin. She could go back. Somehow she could go on with her life. But she would never forget him. Never. "Good luck, Jed." She was proud of her steady voice.

"So long, Cactus. And thanks." For a second or two he looked at her, and she saw a flicker of pain in his eyes, then he gave her a bleak smile and walked steadily to the door with the sheriff at his side.

"I'm going with them," Wayne said grimly, and charged across the room after them.

"Well," Sarah said, her voice sounding strained. "I'm sure Jed didn't mean what he said."

Kristi looked at her, and saw the confusion on her lovely face. She knew what she had to do, and it was the toughest thing she'd ever have to do. But Jed needed Sarah right now, and as much as Kristi hated to admit it, they belonged together. She had to give Sarah the freedom to go to him.

The two of them were alone in the big room now,

and there was no one but Sarah to hear the words that broke her heart. "He meant it, Sarah. We're not really married. We were only pretending to be to give Jed some respectability. He was hoping people, and especially his family, would be more willing to listen to him if they thought he'd settled down with a wife." She shook her head. "I always did think it was a dumb idea."

"No." Sarah looked stricken. "Oh, Kristi, I'm so sorry. I had no idea."

Kristi shrugged. "Well, I guess it was worth a shot."

"It was a wonderful gesture on your part. It couldn't have been easy for you."

"It wasn't." She drew in a deep breath. "It's never easy to see a good friend dealing with the problems Jed was. I just hope things turn out fine for him."

"They will." Sarah laid a hand on her shoulder. "I'll see to it, Kristi. Please try not to worry."

Kristi nodded. "Well, the good news is that Rory more or less admitted he was the one who robbed the gas station. That should clear Jed's name in the town."

Sarah's eyes widened. "Rory confessed?"

"Well, not exactly." Kristi gave her a brief recount of her conversation with Boomer and the exchange that led Rory to incriminate himself.

Sarah shook her head in disbelief when Kristi finished her explanation. "That man. It scares me to think I've been living with a beast like that all these years. I don't think I ever really loved him, though."

She had to ask. "So why did you marry him, then?"

Sarah shrugged. "I was in shock when Jed was arrested. Rory can be very persuasive. He said people might believe I helped Jed if they thought I was hung up on him. He convinced me that if I got engaged to him it would put the suspicions to rest. Then when my parents were killed, Rory was really all I had left. He offered me security, and at the time I wasn't very good at taking care of myself. I know better now."

It really didn't matter anyway, Kristi thought wearily. Now Sarah had Jed to take care of her. She felt exhausted. All she wanted now was to go back to the hotel and try to sleep. To try to forget for a little while all the pain that awaited her tomorrow.

She opened her purse and took out the little package she'd been carrying around with her. "Would you please give this to Jed for me, and wish him a merry Christmas."

Sarah took it with a smile. "Of course. Give me your phone number, too. I'll let you know how things work out."

Kristi shook her head. "I really don't know where I'm going to be."

Sarah gave her a direct look. "I see. Are you sure you want to do this?"

Kristi used the last of her flagging spirits to summon a smile. "I'm sure. Good luck, Sarah. I hope you'll both be very happy."

Sarah's answering smile looked wistful. "So do I. Take care, Kristi. I won't forget you."

Kristi turned away, vowing just the opposite. The

sooner she could forget Sarah Madison the better. As for Jed, he was carved into her heart, and there he would stay until the day she died.

Jed lay on the hard, narrow bed in the county jail, trying to shut out the memory of Kristi's face when he'd sent her away. She'd made a real good try at looking as if she wasn't hurting, but he knew her well enough to know what that effort had cost her.

He rolled over onto his back and stared at the cold, dark ceiling. He was hurting pretty bad himself. But he'd had no choice. He'd screwed up again, and he wasn't about to drag her down with him.

All these years he'd fought the stigma that Rory Madison's treachery had handed him. And now he was back where he started. It hadn't taken very much, after all, to reduce him to the hotheaded rebel who thought he could solve everything with his fists. He hadn't changed at all, and although he was proud of earning the all-around championship, it wasn't going to change who he really was underneath. He was never going to escape his background. No matter what he did, as long as he lived, he'd always be the troublemaker from the wrong side of the tracks.

As for Kristi, he couldn't drag her through all this. She'd agreed to come to Promise as a favor to him. Sooner or later she'd have ended up being tarred with the same brush he was, and he wasn't about to let that happen. She didn't know what it was like to be shunned by people. That kind of hurt went deep. That kind of hurt you never really forgot. Kristi Ramsett deserved better. He could only hope that one day she would forgive him.

Even though she was emotionally exhausted, Kristi spent a sleepless night alone at the hotel. The room seemed so empty without the sound of Jed's even breathing, and creak of the bedsprings when he turned over. By the morning the ache in her heart was almost too much to bear.

She showered, then packed her bags and Jed's as well. She had given Jed more than a tie for a Christmas present. With any luck she'd given him back his life. She had to be content with that. Now she had a few things she needed to settle in her own life. It was time to say goodbye to Promise, Arizona and to the one man in the world she could ever love.

Chapter 11

Kristi did her best over the Christmas holidays to hide her broken heart. Her father seemed happy to see her, and was more animated than she ever remembered seeing him. Since she couldn't take all the credit for that, she had to assume that the prospect of retiring really excited him.

She was pleased when he suggested they attend the Christmas service in the little church where she'd celebrated so many holidays when she was growing up. Before that, however, she told him, she wanted to visit her mother's grave.

She was a little disappointed when he made an excuse not to go with her, but once she reached the granite headstone that marked the place where her mother was buried, she was glad of the opportunity to spend a few moments there alone.

She knelt in the biting wind, with snowflakes

dancing around her face, and placed her small wreath of holly at the head of the grave. She hadn't talked to her mother's spirit in a good many years, but the urge to do so now was too strong to ignore. "I miss you, Mom," she whispered. "I missed you all those years when I was growing up without you in my life. I miss you now, especially. Dad is selling the stockyards, and the house with it. He wanted so badly to keep the business in the family, but I guess he doesn't trust me not to run it into the ground."

She traced her fingers along the lettering that spelled her mother's name. "Oh, Mom, why couldn't I have been the boy he wanted? Or the woman that Jed wanted? I miss Jed so much. I wish you could have met him, Mom. I wish he could have loved me the way I love him."

The snowflakes melted on her cheeks, and she touched them with her fingers. Except they weren't snowflakes after all. And, for the first time since she'd first knelt by this grave all those years ago, Kristi Ramsett cried.

The little church was crowded when she and her father entered it later that morning. Looking around, Kristi saw many familiar faces, and most people greeted her with a wave and a smile. How different from the way Jed was treated when he went back to Promise, she thought wistfully, then chided herself for dwelling on a subject she'd promised herself to forget.

She enjoyed the service, comforted by the familiar warm walls and stained-glass windows, the ageless carols and the feeling of being part of a close-knit community. She had missed that so much when she was on the circuit, and it was always a joy to come back home. Only it wasn't going to be her home for very much longer, she reminded herself as she filed out behind her father into the cold, crisp air of an Oregon winter.

"Kristi? How nice to see you!"

An elderly woman waved a fur-clad hand, and Kristi recognized a neighbor of her father's. "Mrs. Harrison!" She waved back.

The woman trotted over to her, her face wreathed in smiles. "Kristi, how good to see you back in town. How long are you staying?"

"I haven't really decided yet," Kristi answered, with a quick glance at her father. She wasn't sure if her father had told everyone he was selling out, and she wasn't about to be the first one to break the news. Ramsett Stockyards had been around almost as long as the town had existed.

"Well, I'm surprised you haven't brought a husband home with you yet," the other woman said chattily. "I keep hoping to see you with a couple of little ones by your side. I suppose one day we'll see that happen."

"No," Kristi said quietly. "I really don't think so. I have no intention of ever getting married." She gave her father a meaningful look. "We really should be running along if you want that turkey at a reasonable hour."

Mrs. Harrison nodded. "Well, merry Christmas, my dear, and don't stay away so long next time."

"I'll try not to." Kristi smiled at the woman, and waited until she was out of earshot before saying to her father, "I take it you haven't announced the sale of the stockyards."

"Not until they're sold. It could take some time to find the right buyer and I don't want to start any anxious speculation on what might become of the land."

She looked at him anxiously. "You are going to make sure the stockyards will stay?"

He nodded. "I promise. I wouldn't want to see a factory or a subdivision on that land."

Satisfied with his answer, she followed him over to the car. They had barely pulled out onto the road before her father surprised her by saying, "What was all that about back there?"

For a moment she was bewildered. "All what?"

"All that stuff about never getting married. Is there something I should know?"

"Not really. I guess I'm just not the kind of woman men want to marry, that's all."

"That's nonsense," her father said firmly. "Whatever put that fool idea into your head?"

She sighed. "Look at me. I'm thirty years old, and I've never had anyone propose to me."

"That's because you spent so much of your time running around with a bunch of cowboys who thought you were one of them. You sure as hell looked the part."

Surprised that he'd even noticed, she said tartly, "You surely don't expect me to wrestle in the mud with the heifers wearing a fancy dress and high heels?''

"Aw, it wasn't just the clothes, Kristi. It was everything. The way you walked, and the way you talked…sometimes I wondered if I'd fathered a girl or a boy.''

She tightened her mouth. "You seem to have it straight now.''

"That's because you've changed, Kristi. A lot. I don't know why or how, but I like it. You're finally dressing like a woman. You look like a woman—hell, you've even lost that tough, rowdy way of talking. I haven't heard you cuss once since you came home. Now, if you'd done that to yourself ten years ago, you might have been married and given me grandkids by now.''

It was the last straw. The pain of all she'd lost seemed to crush her like a careless hand crumpling a rose petal. In her agony she lashed out, heedless of the stricken expression on her father's face.

"Damn it, Dad, if I've been looking and acting like a man all my life it's entirely your fault. You never let me forget the fact that you were disappointed you didn't have a son. I spent my life trying to be that damn son you wanted so much. After Mom died, you were all I had, and all I wanted was to be a part of your life.''

"But you were, Kristi. You have always *been* my life.''

She gave a fierce shake of her head. "No, I wasn't. I tried…oh, God, how I tried. Instead of ballet lessons and ice-skating I was learning how to muck out

a stable and birth a cow. I got my bruises learning
how to ride, and I didn't give up until I could ride
as well as any of the stock handlers. I figured the
tougher I was, the more chance I had of making you
realize I was as good as any of them. But you
couldn't see that, could you? I might as well have
stuck to the dancing and ice-skating. I was a girl, and
that was all you saw. And now you're selling the
stockyards. The business that should have been mine.
The home that should have been mine, because you
can't trust me enough to run it as well as you did.
And that's what hurts most of all."

"Now, hold on one cotton-picking minute." Paul
Ramsett brought the car to a standstill alongside the
road.

Kristi felt sick. She hadn't meant to spill all that
out. On Christmas Day of all times. What the hell
was the matter with her? "Sorry, Dad," she muttered. "I guess I'm a little stressed out right now.
Just forget what I said."

"No," her father said quietly. "I'm glad you told
me. I didn't realize what was going on, and for that
I'm really sorry." He let out a long sigh, then turned
in his seat to face her. "Kristi...honey...I just wish
you could see yourself right now. You look so much
like your mom when she was your age that it breaks
my heart to look at you. Maybe that's why I didn't
pay you the attention you deserved. It hurt too much
to see you growing more like your mom every day.
It just tore me apart."

"Oh, God. I'm so sorry—"

"No." He held up his hand. "Let me finish. I was

wrong, and I'm the one who's sorry. You are your mother's daughter, Kristi. A carbon copy of her. That means more to me than any son could. I'm so very proud of you, for all you've achieved. It was tough on you, I know, growing up without a mother, and not much of a father, I guess. But you've grown into an incredible woman, in spite of all that. You're smart, you're beautiful, and you're one hell of a horsewoman. I don't know what I would have done without you all these years. No one could have done a better job. Man or woman. And I really mean that.''

"Thank you." She smiled, hoping that the lump in her throat didn't mean she was going to cry again.

Paul Ramsett looked down at the wheel. "Maybe we didn't spend much time together, Kristi, but you were always there for me when I needed you, and that's what counted with me. As for the stockyards, I figured I was doing the right thing by selling up. I didn't want to saddle you with the business when you have so much of your life to live yet. I guess I was afraid that if I offered you the stockyards, you'd be tied up with that for life and then you'd never get married.''

"But that doesn't matter...."

"It does matter, Kristi. I want to see you married. I want to you to be as happy as I was with your mother for those all-too-brief years. I want grand-children—lots of them. If there's a grandson among them, I'll be the happiest man on earth. And if they're all granddaughters, I reckon I'll be just as happy. That's why I want to sell the stockyards, honey. Not because I think you're incapable of running them, but because I felt it was the best thing for you and your happiness.''

She swallowed, hard. ''Didn't you ever think of asking me what I want?''

He looked worried. ''Well, I was kind of hoping it was the same thing. Don't all women want to end up happily married with kids of their own?''

She managed a shaky laugh. ''Not all of them, Dad.''

''But you do, don't you?''

She shrugged. ''I thought I did. I guess it just isn't in the cards for me.''

''Aw, hell, Kristi, it's never too late to find yourself a good man. Now that you've turned out to be such a pretty lady, you're gonna have to fight 'em off.''

She would have laughed again if she hadn't remembered someone else saying something similar. *I thought I'd stake my claim before I have to fight them all off.* Jed's words, the first time they'd danced at Cord's wedding. Jed, with his teasing smile and laughing golden eyes. She shut off the bittersweet memory and concentrated on what her father was saying.

''As a matter of fact, I guess it isn't too late for me, either. I've met someone, Kristi. Someone who I believe can make me happy. She'll never replace your mom, of course, but she's a sweet lady, and I'd like to spend whatever years I've got left with her.''

Genuinely happy for him, she laid her hand on his arm. ''That's wonderful, Dad. When do I get to meet her?''

"Well, I wasn't going to tell you until I asked the lady, but I intend to propose on New Year's Eve. If she accepts, I'd like to bring her back to the house for a little celebration, if that's okay with you."

"Of course it's okay with me." She leaned in and kissed him on the cheek. "Congratulations, Dad. And of course she'll accept. She'd be a fool to turn down such a great catch."

He made a face. "I don't know about that, but I really care for her a lot. I hope you will, too."

"If you chose her, then I know I'll love her, too." She patted his arm. "Let's go home and celebrate."

He grinned at her. "Hell, let's go home and cook that turkey. I'm starving."

"So that's where I get it from," she murmured.

"What?"

"Never mind." She made herself smile. "Merry Christmas, Dad."

"Merry Christmas, honey. And welcome home. I'm so glad you could come."

"So am I." And this time she meant it.

She cooked the turkey that afternoon, and exchanged gifts with her father. He talked about Diana, the woman he intended to ask to be his wife, and Kristi listened, aware that she and her father seemed closer now than at any time in her life. They shared the Christmas meal, and her father told her stories about the times she was too young to remember, before her mother died.

The hours, and eventually the days slipped by, and not for one second could she escape the empty ache in her heart, or the longing for the man who had put it there. So many times she was tempted to call Sarah, but she knew she couldn't bear to hear that the two of them were happy together.

On New Year's Eve she watched her father leave for his momentous dinner date. She spent the evening in front of a roaring fire, trying to make sense of a mystery novel she'd found in her father's bookcase. Images of Jed kept intruding, and after a while she gave it up and switched on the television.

The ringing of the phone woke her from her nap in the comfortable armchair. She glanced at the clock, wryly noting that she'd slept through the new year. It was fifteen minutes past midnight.

Her father's jubilant voice greeted her when she answered the phone. "She said yes!" he shouted. "I'm getting married again."

She pressed her lips together and blinked hard. "That's wonderful, Dad. Congratulations. I'm so happy for you both."

"Is it too late to come home for a glass of champagne, or are you too tired?"

"Of course not," Kristi said brightly. "I'm dying to meet her." Just a couple more hours, she promised herself. She could give her father that much. But then she had to leave. She had a new life to start.

Diana turned out to be a soft-spoken, motherly type of woman, and Kristi fell in love with her right away. She wasn't at all surprised when her father informed her that Diana would be staying for the night.

By the time her father came down the next morning, Kristi was packed and ready to go.

"Diana's still sleeping," he explained, avoiding her eyes. "I thought we'd have breakfast together. I'm starving."

She smiled. "So am I." She cooked bacon and scrambled eggs and laid places for them at the small dinette table in the kitchen.

"I have something for you," her father said, as she sat down to eat. "I wanted to give it to you before Diana comes down."

Puzzled, she took the sheaf of pages he handed her. She leafed through them, her eyes widening in amazement when she read the official notice that Paul Ramsett was handing over the reins of the business to his daughter.

The words blurred together and she hastily blinked. How long she had wanted this! It was all she'd ever dreamed about. But now that she was actually holding her dream in her hands, it felt hollow and empty. She couldn't stay in contact with the rodeo. Now that Jed was champion, he'd be highly visible.

She would have to check out the handlers from time to time. Especially at first, until she'd trained a competent assistant. She was bound to run into Jed, and each time would be death to any hopes of getting over him. She just couldn't watch him with Sarah. Not even for the stockyards.

She handed the papers back to her father. "I'm sorry, Dad, but I can't accept this. I thought a lot about what you said, about the business getting in the way of my life and what I wanted to do, and you were right. I need to do something more with my life, and now that I have a new image and a new outlook I want to see how far it will take me.''

He looked disappointed, but not terribly surprised. ''I figured that's what you'd say. But I wanted you to know it's yours, if you'd wanted it.''

She nodded. ''Thanks, Dad. That means a lot to me.''

He cleared his throat. ''Kristi, whoever he is, don't let him break your heart. There are a lot of good men out there, just waiting for the right woman to come along.''

She stared at him. ''How did you know?''

He shrugged. ''You're my daughter. I know when you're hurting. I just put two and two together.''

She gave him a bleak smile and stood up, her arms outstretched for a hug. ''I'll be okay,'' she whispered.

''I hope so. I want those grandkids.''

She stepped back and punched him on the shoulder. ''Just make sure you and Diana are happy, all right?''

''I intend to.''

''I'll keep you to that.'' She sat down again. ''Now let's eat this before it gets any colder. I'm starving.''

She left that afternoon, after her father and Diana had given her an emotional farewell at the bus terminal. The next day she was in her camper, heading for Seattle. She found a job with a riding school, and a modest apartment that had its drawbacks but was cheap enough for her to manage.

She gave away all her fancy clothes to Goodwill, and went back to wearing jeans. Feeling more like her old self again, she soon settled into her new routine, and although the ache never left her, its bite had tempered a bit by the time the first crocuses poked their heads warily through the hard winter crust.

It was a blustery, damp morning when her father called her to announce that he had sold the stockyards and the house. She did her best to sound enthusiastic, but she knew he wasn't fooled. Now that she was faced with the reality of it, the loss of her home and the business was tougher to take than she'd anticipated.

"How are things going?" Paul Ramsett asked, when she'd finished congratulating him on the sale.

She sensed something guarded in his tone and frowned. "Are you okay, Dad? You're not sick, are you? You haven't broken up with Diana?"

He laughed. "No, honey, as matter of fact, that's one of the reasons I called. I want to invite you to the wedding in June."

"I wouldn't miss it for the world," Kristi said unsteadily.

"Diana was wondering if you'd be her bridesmaid. She doesn't have any family, and she thought it would be nice if you would do this for her."

Kristi closed her eyes, remembering the last time she'd been a bridesmaid. "I'd love it," she assured him. "It would be an honor."

"Good, then that's settled."

"So what's the new owner like?" Kristi asked, wondering what it was her father was holding back. "He is going to keep the stockyards, isn't he?"

"You bet he is. He seems like a real capable guy." Her father hesitated. "You are sure about this, aren't you?"

She made a real effort to sound convincing. "Yes, of course. I agree with you, it's the right thing to do. We both have new lives now, and we have to move on."

"Yes, I thought so." Her father cleared his throat. "Well, honey, I have to run. I'll be in touch with you soon."

She said goodbye and hung up. So it was over. The last of her ties with the rodeo were cut.

In spite of her determination to fight it, her depression grew deeper throughout the long day. Her head throbbed, and it didn't help when one of her charges screamed in protest when it was time to get off the horse. It took all of Kristi's patience to persuade the child to dismount and go back to the office with her.

She arrived at her apartment complex wondering if she should look for another line of work. She certainly wasn't enjoying what she was doing. As she walked across the parking lot she caught sight of a tall man hovering near the entrance to her building. He wore a cowboy hat, and as always, her insides clenched as the pain of remembering sliced into her again.

She had to stop this, she told herself. She couldn't fall apart every time she saw a man wearing a cowboy hat. She tried not to look at him as she approached, but when she was a few feet away from him he turned, and took a step toward her.

The world rocked crazily, and her stomach seemed to drop like a stone.

"Hi," Jed said, tipping his hat back with his thumb. "I thought you were never going to get here. I'm starving."

She stared at him, still unable to believe he was really standing there with the familiar grin splitting his face, and not a figment of her imagination. Unable to suppress the leap of joy she felt at seeing him, she demanded huskily, "What are you doing here? How did you know where to find me?"

"Your father told me. I went to see him."

"My father?" No wonder he'd sounded guarded on the phone this morning, she thought grimly. She couldn't imagine why Jed had gone to the trouble of finding her, and she refused to respond to the flicker of hope. She'd been down that street too many times.

"Yeah." Jed rubbed the wet sleeves of his jacket with his hands. "Can we go in? It's darn cold waiting around in this rain."

She didn't want him in her apartment. She'd made a new life for herself there, and he didn't belong in it. Yet she knew how impossible it would be to refuse him. "I hope you're not looking forward to a steak. All I have in the fridge is hamburger."

"Hamburger sounds great."

She steeled herself to look into his eyes, hoping for some clue as to why he was there. But he was turning away from her, already heading for the entrance. She followed him, determined not to let anything as stupid as wishing for the impossible shatter the hard shell she'd built around her heart.

"Nice," he said, when she let him into the apartment. "This must seem huge after the camper."

"It does and it is." She dropped her coat on a chair and crossed to the kitchen, her nerves tightening when he followed her.

"Where is the camper, anyway? I didn't see it in the parking lot. I thought I might have the wrong address at first."

She filled the coffeepot with water, her hand not quite steady. "I sold it. I didn't need it anymore." She glanced over her shoulder at him. "I'm making coffee, but I have beer if you'd prefer that."

"Coffee's fine."

He sat down at her kitchen table, making it look ridiculously small. Even now it was hard to convince herself he was there, in her apartment, and that she wasn't having a particularly vivid dream.

"So, how's the new job going?" he asked, as she reached for the coffee mugs in the cupboard above the dishwasher.

"Good," she said cheerfully. "I love working with the kids, and every day is different. It's quite a challenge. But how about you? What happened about the assault charges?"

"Rory dropped the charges. He didn't have much choice after the newspapers made such a big deal out of the fight. I reckon everyone knows now what he did."

She turned to face him, thrilled that it had all

turned out so right. "Oh, Jed, I'm so happy for you. What about your father? What did he say when he found out?"

"He doesn't say much about anything as a rule. He did apologize, though." Jed smiled. "That's the first time I ever heard him say he was sorry."

Kristi sat down at the table. "I'm sure he was. Your mom must be happy for you, too."

"I guess."

She wanted so badly to give him a hug. "You did it, J. C. You finally got what you wanted."

"Maybe."

Something in his voice disturbed her. "What do you mean, maybe?"

"Well, you know how it is with the Madisons. Rory's still strutting around town like nothing happened."

"He should pay for what he did," Kristi said hotly. "After everything he'd done to you. How is he going to make up for that?"

Jed shook his head. "There's nothing I want from him. Anyway, I reckon he's paying for it now. He's lost the town's respect. He'll have a tough time dealing with that."

She got up as the last of the water dripped through the coffee filter. "Did he ever say what really happened that night?"

"He didn't. But once Gary read about it in the paper he couldn't wait to tell everyone what he knew. I reckon he was afraid of being booked for perjury."

"So what did happen?"

"Pretty much what I thought. Rory was gonna

frame me by making it look as if I'd broken into the
gas station. He was going to break in the door, then
he figured on calling the sheriff the next day to tell
him he saw someone breaking in wearing a mask and
to look for it in my backyard. Only he didn't figure
on Boomer being there. He had the gun in his jacket
pocket and he used it to knock Boomer out before
he recognized him. Then he got scared. He thought
he'd killed the guy. So he buried the gun and the
mask in our backyard, figuring if it was ever found,
I'd be the one who got arrested for the murder.''

Kristi tightened her lips. ''Nice man.''

''Yeah. Anyway, when Rory found out that
Boomer wasn't dead, after all, he called the sheriff
and told him where to find the gun and the mask.
Then he spoke to Dave and Gary to persuade them
to lie for him. I guess he told them that if they gave
him an alibi, he'd make sure they'd be on 'easy
street' for the rest of their lives. Dave found the key
after Rory had left, and the rest you know.''

Kristi handed him the mug of coffee and sat down
opposite him. She'd deliberately avoided asking
about Sarah, but now she could put it off no longer.
She made an effort to sound offhand. ''And did
Sarah get her divorce?''

''She hired a lawyer, yeah. It's going to take a
while, but she's willing to stay there and fight it out
for as long as it takes.''

''And what about you? You'll be defending your
title next year, won't you?''

''Well, no,'' Jed said slowly. ''I'm figuring on giving up the rodeo circuit. Now that I've made champion, I reckon I'm ready to retire.''

The lump in her throat grew bigger. Of course. He'd want to stay in Promise to be with Sarah. He must love her a lot to give up the rodeo for her. ''You'll miss it,'' she said unsteadily.

''Yeah, I reckon I will.''

''Will you stay in Promise with Sarah?'' She couldn't look at him, though she could feel his gaze intent on her face.

''Sarah's going to New York after the divorce,'' he said quietly. ''She's planning on opening up an antique store. She's got a friend there who's going into business with her.''

Surprise compelled her to look at him. ''How do you feel about that? It's hard to imagine you living in a big city like New York.''

Something in his eyes stilled her breath. ''I'm not going to be living in New York.''

No, she told herself fiercely. Don't start hoping all over again. Her lips felt stiff when she answered. ''I don't understand. I thought that you and Sarah—''

He shot out his hand and trapped her fingers. ''I know what you thought. Sarah told me. You were wrong.''

She looked down at his strong brown hand covering hers. ''I'm sorry. I think Sarah really cares a lot for you.''

''Kristi.''

Heady with the joy of knowing he wasn't going to marry Sarah, she made herself meet his gaze.

"It's good to see you looking like the old Kristi again."

She managed a casual shrug. "All those fancy clothes and high heels were never my style, anyway."

"Well, you looked real good in them, but I kinda missed the spitfire stock handler who wasn't afraid to cuss me out when she had a mind to."

She smiled. "So did I. You know something? I was trying so hard to be someone else for so long, I guess I lost sight of the real me. I'm not a tough wrangler trying to compete with the men, and I'm not a fancy lady like Sarah. I guess I'm somewhere in between, and that's the real me. I have to accept that and be proud of who I am. Good old Kristi Ramsett."

"Well, there's one little change I'd be happy to see you make."

She eyed him warily. "What's that?"

He dropped his gaze, and started rubbing his thumb across the back of her hand in an absent way that told her he was unsure of himself. "I've never done this before," he said, as the hope began to build in her heart. "So bear with me. It's taken me a long time to figure this out, but what I thought was important really isn't worth a damn. I wanted respect, and I thought I could buy it back with a championship buckle. Well, I was wrong. I thought I could show everyone I'd made a success of my life. But gold buckles and a classy wife don't make a man successful. What does make a man successful is the way he treats other people, and the way they treat him. Compassion, integrity, loyalty, those are the things that make a man."

She smiled. "You have all those things, Jed."

"I guess that's really my point. It doesn't matter if you have a rodeo championship, a mansion and a mill, a high-class wife or just a little house on Partridge Creek. It's how you measure up when you look at yourself in the mirror. Well, I took a good long look in that mirror, and I figure I'm gonna do all right. I don't need to prove anything to the people of Promise, Arizona. I just had to prove something to myself."

She smiled at him. "I guess we both had to find that out for ourselves."

"Yeah, well there's one more thing."

Her pulse leapt again with the irrepressible hope. "What's that?"

"Well, I reckon a man's not really complete without a good woman at his side." Gazing at her steadily, he continued, "A woman he loves very much. And maybe a couple of kids. Or three. Or four."

Her hand beneath his began to tremble. "And?" she asked faintly.

"Well, that's why I'm here. I love you, Kristie. And I'd be greatly honored, ma'am, if you'd consider marrying me and raising my sons. And daughters. Both."

"Oh, God." She pressed her free hand to her mouth.

He looked at her anxiously. "Heck, Cactus, you're not going to cry on me, are you?"

"No," she said unsteadily. "But I am going to marry you and raise your sons. And daughters."

His grin was wonderful to see. "Reckon we ought to get started on that right away, seeing as how much time we've missed already."

She didn't need words to tell him what she thought of that suggestion. She only had one thing to say to him. "I love you, Jed Cullen."

Much later, as they lay together in her rumpled bed, he kissed her on the nose, then announced, "Now that we've got all that settled, I've got a wedding present for you."

She gave him a calculating look. "Really. How come you were so sure I'd marry you?"

"Sarah told me you would," he said blithely. "I reckon women know these things."

Kristi knew why she liked Sarah now. "I hope she'll be as happy as we are someday."

Jed grinned. "Anyone who looks like Sarah isn't going to have to wait too long."

"You're right." She sighed.

He bent his head and gave her a long, lingering kiss on the mouth. "Sarah was never the right woman for me," he said when he lifted his head. "I need someone who can keep me in line."

She grinned happily at him. "Then I reckon you've got your woman, J. C."

"Don't I know it."

"So tell me about the wedding present."

"Oh, yeah." He pulled away from her and slipped out of bed.

She watched him cross the floor to where his jacket lay across the chair. She would never get tired of looking at his strong, naked body, she thought dreamily as she watched him pull a long envelope from his pocket and carry it back to her.

She took it from him, turning it over in her hands. "What's this?"

"Open it."

Intrigued, she slid her thumb under the flap and slit the envelope open. Inside she found a single sheet of paper. She unfolded it and read the words typed there, trying to make sense of what she saw. "This is an agreement to buy the Ramsett Stockyards."

"Yep."

She stared at him, afraid to think what it might mean. "Jed, how did you get this?"

"I bought it!" He took the paper from her nerveless hand and showed her the signatures at the bottom. "Look, there I am. Jedrow P. Cullen, the new owner of Ramsett Stockyards. Well, actually Ramsett and Cullen Stockyards. Or Cullen and Ramsett. I guess we can sort that out lat—"

He was interrupted by a shrill scream as Kristi flung her arms around his neck. "I don't believe it! You own the stockyards? But how? Why?"

He was prevented from answering for a moment while she smothered him with kisses. Finally, when he could speak again, he said huskily, "Well, heck, sweetheart, if we're gonna raise sons and daughters I sure want something bigger than a camper."

"But won't you miss the rodeos?"

"Nope. Not as long as I'm raising stock for

them.'' He crinkled his eyes at her. ''Of course, I'm gonna need your help in running the business. You know a lot more about it than I do. I figure you're happy with that?''

''You bet I'm happy with that.'' Life, she thought, as she gazed at her beloved husband-to-be, was suddenly incredibly good. ''Now, let's go get something to eat. I'm starving.''

* * * * *

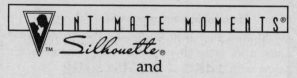

If you enjoyed what you just read,
then we've got an offer you can't resist!

Take 2 bestselling
love stories FREE!

Plus get a FREE surprise gift!

Clip this page and mail it to Silhouette Reader Service™

IN U.S.A.	**IN CANADA**
3010 Walden Ave.	P.O. Box 609
P.O. Box 1867	Fort Erie, Ontario
Buffalo, N.Y. 14240-1867	L2A 5X3

YES! Please send me 2 free Silhouette Intimate Moments® novels and my free surprise gift. Then send me 6 brand-new novels every month, which I will receive months before they're available in stores. In the U.S.A., bill me at the bargain price of $3.57 plus 25¢ delivery per book and applicable sales tax, if any*. In Canada, bill me at the bargain price of $3.96 plus 25¢ delivery per book and applicable taxes**. That's the complete price and a savings of over 10% off the cover prices—what a great deal! I understand that accepting the 2 free books and gift places me under no obligation ever to buy any books. I can always return a shipment and cancel at any time. Even if I never buy another book from Silhouette, the 2 free books and gift are mine to keep forever. So why not take us up on our invitation. You'll be glad you did!

245 SEN CNFF

345 SEN CNFG

Name _____ (PLEASE PRINT)

Address _____ Apt.# _____

City _____ State/Prov. _____ Zip/Postal Code _____

* Terms and prices subject to change without notice. Sales tax applicable in N.Y.
** Canadian residents will be charged applicable provincial taxes and GST.
   All orders subject to approval. Offer limited to one per household.
   ® are registered trademarks of Harlequin Enterprises Limited.

INMOM99   ©1998 Harlequin Enterprises Limited

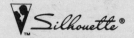

SILHOUETTE BOOKS
is proud to announce the arrival of

THE BABY OF THE MONTH CLUB:

BABY TALK

the latest installment of author
Marie Ferrarella's
popular miniseries.

When pregnant Juliette St. Claire met Gabriel Saldana than she discovered he wasn't the struggling artist he claimed to be. An undercover agent, Gabriel had been sent to Juliette's gallery to nab his prime suspect: Juliette herself. But when he discovered her innocence, would he win back Juliette's heart and convince her that he was the daddy her baby needed?

Don't miss Juliette's induction into
THE BABY OF THE MONTH CLUB
in September 1999.
Available at your favorite retail outlet.

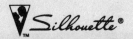

Silhouette®

"Fascinating—you'll want to take this home!"
—**Marie Ferrarella**

"Each page is filled with a brand-new surprise."
—**Suzanne Brockmann**

"Makes reading a new and joyous experience all over again."
—**Tara Taylor Quinn**

See what all your favorite authors are talking about.

Coming October 1999 to a retail store near you.

HARLEQUIN®
Makes any time special ™

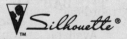

Silhouette®